Because of Roses

Richard May

Spectrum Books

Artwork: Adobe Stock – © Budimir Jevtic.

Cover designed by Spectrum Books.

Paperback ISBN: 978-1-915905-07-9

First edition, Spectrum Books, 2023

Discover more LGBTQ+ books at www.spectrum-books.com

Contents

"Because of Roses" from NEVER TOO LATE (Dreamspinner Press, 2015)

"Chicken Man" An earlier 3000-word version published in Indie Writers' Deathmatch 2018 (Broken Pencil Magazine)

"The Green Bench" from OUTER VOICES INNER LIVES (MadeMark Publishing, 2014)

"Leprechaun in New York" from INHUMAN BEINGS (MLR Press, 2016)

"Ticket to Ride" from INHUMAN BEINGS (MLR Press, 2016)

For my life partner,
Wayne Goodman,
who gives me roses every year

Chicken Man

Coming up Broadway was a tall man wearing yellow spandex and a rooster's head. Other than that, he was quite attractive. Yummy legs, delicious thighs, and meaty breasts.

The chicken spoke to me in a human voice. "Hey, buddy, where is 213 West 49th?" I pointed uptown. "Thanks, man," he said and continued on his roosterly way. The rear view was just as mouthwatering as the front. After a few steps though, Chicken Man stopped and turned around.

"Com'ere," he said, one finger beckoning. "What's your name?"

I had never exchanged contact information with a chicken before. "Carl," I answered, my voice squawking. The chicken's aquamarine eyes looked me up and down.

"How tall are you?" he asked.

"Five eight," I said, trying not to stammer.

"Five eight," Chicken Man mused in a non-avian way. "Might be a stretch." He laughed as if he'd made a joke. I thought I better laugh too, just in case, but he frowned, so I stopped.

"What are you doing?" he asked.

I started backing away. "Nothing. I'm sorry I bothered you."

He grimaced. "No, I mean now."

"Now?" I repeated stupidly.

"No, yesterday. Yeah, now and for the next five days."

"Nothing," I said, because it was true. I had been in New York three months and was still waiting for my big showbiz break.

"Let's go," he said. He grabbed my hand and took off up Broadway, walking fast.

"Wait a minute!" I yelled, trying to delay his forward motion. "Where are we going? I don't even know who you are!"

The chicken stopped, removed his rooster mask, and extended a human hand. I couldn't stop staring at his black hair, blue eyes, and two-day beard.

"Sorry. I'm Hinkel," he said, hand still out.

"Hinkel?"

He dropped his hand. "Yeah, Hinkel. Got a problem with that?" I could see myself about to be pounded into the sidewalk outside McDonald's, so I shook my head vigorously *no* several times. "Okay, then," he said with a kind of grunt, and we resumed walking at Hinkel speed, which meant we reached 213 West 49th Street in what seemed like seconds, especially since Hinkel ignored stoplights and cut in between cabs and delivery trucks blocking the box.

The building was one of those low, narrow ones in the Theater District you know are headed for skyscraper replacement. Hinkel walked us past reception, carrying his rooster mask. The guard didn't even look up.

A small elevator was waiting. We squeezed ourselves in, and Hinkel pressed the ninth-floor button. His thigh squashed against mine like we were inside the same spandex. The thirty-something women already in the elevator stared at Hinkel, then at his rooster head, and then at me. I tried to smile, but they looked away like they'd seen it all.

"What do you do?" Hinkel asked me conversationally as the elevator creaked up a floor and let one of the women off.

"I'm an actor?" I answered-asked. I was still getting used to saying the words.

"Perfect!" he said way too enthusiastically, spraying me with the *ffffffft*.

"Why?" I asked, wiping my face with the back of my hand as we reached the fourth floor, where the second woman exited. The doors closed behind her with a bang. Chicken Man and I were now alone. I started praying the elevator would break down. Hinkel leaned against the back wall of the lift, displaying himself. I wanted to lean against Hinkel.

"I've got a gig for you, Carl."

Now *I* was enthusiastic. "Really? What is it?"

"You'll see. This is us. Get out." The doors opened and Hinkel muscled me through them. "This way," he said, putting his hand on my back and steering me right.

His hand guided me down a narrow hallway with dark wood paneling on either side. The floor was tiled in an appropriate chicken-wire pattern. We passed lines of heavy oak doors with opaque glass windows at eye level, names of miscellaneous companies painted on them, until we came to a door which read "Marx Novelty Acts." Hinkel turned the doorknob and ushered me in.

A receptionist with purple hair and blue lips welcomed us. "The chicken!" she exclaimed before looking suspiciously at me. "Where's the hen?" she asked.

"This is him," Hinkel replied, with just a little uncertainty in his Queens accent.

The vision in purple and blue narrowed her eyes at him. "Hens are not hims, Hinkel. Where is she?"

"Look, Marlene, my girlfriend got sick. I couldn't find anybody else. This guy can do it. He's an actor. Tell her, Carl."

"I'm an actor," I agreed. Chicken Man looked at me, disgusted. I didn't care. The word *girlfriend* had diluted my interest in him and his "gig."

"Hinkel, Mr. Marx is not going to like this."

"He here?"

"Not yet. 20 minutes.

"Here, Carlo." My enthusiasm rose a little, hearing his nickname for me. He removed a package from his backpack. "Go change."

I looked around for where. The receptionist stood up, sighing. "In here, I guess," she said, leading me into the inner office. I waited until she left to strip down to my underwear, whereupon Hinkel opened the door, and he and Marlene got a good look at my blue boxers. "Very nice," Marlene yelled before Hinkel closed the door and hustled me out of the boxers and into the hen costume. His strong fingers manhandled me along the way, which I didn't mind at all.

When he finished, the yellow spandex was stretched taut across my body. I might as well have been naked. "How big is your girlfriend?" I asked him.

"She's not really my girlfriend," he muttered. "Anyway, obviously not as big as you. About the same height, though. I thought it would work." He tugged the costume here and there half-heartedly, looking depressed.

About that time, Marlene opened the door again. "Ten minutes," she announced. Her mouth fell open, then closed in a frown. "Uh, Hinkel?" she began. "There's a problem here. Actually, two problems." She poked my chest and grabbed my crotch. I hopped away from her.

Hinkel's eyes lit up. "Quick, Marlene. Give Carlo your bra!"

"What?" the receptionist and I squawked in unison.

"Hurry up!" he said, but Marlene just stood there, her blue mouth hanging open. Without another word, Hinkel hugged her and slid his hands up the back of her blouse. He unhooked the bra in an easy 1-2-3, whipped it off, and tried to hand it to me. "Shirt off! Bra on!" he yelled. The D-cups swung hypnotically in front of my eyes. When I didn't immediately respond, Hinkel yanked the spandex shirt up my chest and over my head. The guy seemed to have considerable experience in speedy removal of clothing.

Marlene ogled my chest. "Nice man-boobs, Carlo," she said, helping me on with the bra and cotching a feel or two along the way.

Hinkel studied the effect. He did not seem pleased. "Gimme your socks," he demanded, and grabbed his own from his backpack. He stuffed one of his and one of mine into each cup and fussed with them until Marlene took over.

When she had me nicely built, she asked, "What about these?" and pointed at my junk bulging obviously in tight and yellow. She licked her lips and gave me a wink.

"Here," Hinkel yelled, whipping off his shoes and wiggling out of his spandex pants. It looked like he was wearing some kind of jockstrap, which, of course, he removed immediately. Marlene and I gasped. Hinkel was a big chicken in more than one way.

"Stop staring and get into this thing!" He threw the apparatus my way.

"What is it?" I asked, trying to figure out how it worked.

"A dancer's belt," Hinkel replied, which told me nothing. But he was approaching with hands ready to assist, so I quickly stepped out of my Converses and started pulling down my spandex pants, thereby uncovering my half-erection. Marlene's eyes bugged, and my face started burning.

"Oh, sweet Jesus, Mary, and Joseph!" Hinkel shouted in disgust. "Marlene, Carlo's shy. You gotta leave!"

Marlene's eyes reluctantly left my crotch. "Uh, okay. But hurry. Mr. M will be here any minute." The second she was gone, Hinkel was pulling my pants off the rest of the way and helping me into the dancer thingee. When he fit the back strap between my ass cheeks, my erection went full vertical.

"Damn, Carlo! You gotta stuff that thing down!" When he tried to do the stuffing for me, I jumped so high I nearly hit the ceiling fan. I pushed him away and got my 'thing' down on my own. We had just stuck our rooster and hen heads on when a fiftyish man with a greying goatee breezed into the inner office, followed by an apprehensive-looking Marlene.

"My chickens!" he yelled at us in greeting. He looked at me appraisingly. "So, this is the girlfriend?" he asked, with one hand on his hip and the other rubbing his chin. Hinkel nodded. "Nice boobs, lady. Sorry, man, I had you pegged as queer. Okay, Marlene, you got their stuff ready?" Marlene nodded, relief all over her face. "Okay, sit down, chickens. Can you sit in spandex? Geez, I can see everything you got. Almost." He gave me a wink. Marlene gave my buns a prolonged squeeze while Mr. Marx took a seat behind at his desk.

"Marlene, when you're done feeling up the hen's tush, would you please get their bags?" She hurried into the reception area and returned with two Macy's Big Bags. I took a look in one. It was full of leaflets.

"Okay, let's go over this," Marx said. "You two are promoting the opening of the first Chicken on a Stick franchise in Manhattan. This is big." He spread his hands wide for emphasis. "You'll be handing out these free Single Stick cards in Times Square and directing people to the franchise location in Port Authority every day this week, 8 to 5. Got it? Oh, yeah. One card to a customer."

I nodded my chicken head.

"How do we get paid?" Hinkel asked through his.

"By the card. You hand out all the cards, you and the hen split $200 a day, which is good money." He peered over his glasses with a look that dared us to deny it. "But don't go dumping cards in trash cans. You come back early; I'll know."

Some money this week, as opposed to no money, sounded all right to me, and at least I was acting. Sort of. Hinkel, though, was not satisfied. He asked for more. Marx just shook his head. After a staredown, Hinkel stood up and said, "Okay, Carlo. Let's hit it."

"Yeah, *Carla*," Marlene emphasized, looking at Hinkel and swatting my ass. "Get those cute little chicken buns moving."

Marx saw the swat. "What is it with you and the hen's butt, Marlene? Are you turning lesbian on me?"

Marlene just tossed her purple hair at him and flounced out of the room ahead of us. Hinkel asked if he could leave his backpack behind her desk. "No problem, Chicken Man, but remember, I'm out of this dump at 5 p.m. and no seconds."

She winked at me. "Just in time for happy hour." I left quickly, Hinkel close behind me.

The elevator came fast and empty. On the way down, Hinkel kept staring at my chicken breasts. "Your tits do look good," he finally said, his eyes still on them.

"They're socks," I reminded him.

He ignored me and smirked. "But ol' Marlene likes your ass more." He took a look at it. "I can see why." I was pondering his review of my physical attributes—natural and not—when we touched down and the doors opened. A crowd was waiting, but they didn't seem to notice we were chickens as they rushed into the elevator. Outside, back on the street, it was a different story. We got doubletakes, stares, and plenty of comments—including sexual come-ons from straight men (me) and salacious ogles from women and gay men (Hinkel). Guys kept staring at my boobs. I decided tomorrow I'd use only one pair of socks.

Hinkel and I made our way south to Times Square and picked a heavily traversed spot. We worked back-to-back, so we could get people coming and going, and every once in a while, we bumped chicken butts. Hinkel's felt mighty good against mine. I could have handed out free Single Stick cards forever butt to butt with Hinkel, but we ran out by 4:30, so we did the chicken dance back to the Marx Novelty Acts office. We were used to the stares and comments by then.

Mr. Marx expressed pride in our first day's work. He stared at my boobs while he spoke. "You guys are good. Maybe I should get more cards. Anyway, here's your money. See ya tomorrow." When he handed me my twenties, his fingers lingered. Suddenly, I agreed with Hinkel. $100 was not enough.

But Marx left, so Hinkel and I stripped down in his office. Marlene was checking her watch every three seconds. I got the top and bottom of the costume off, but was having trouble with the bra. Hinkel was already naked, which was probably distracting me.

"Here, lemme do that," he said, moving close behind me. In two seconds, the bra was in his hands. I stepped out of his dancer's belt on my own, and my cock started going up like the elevator. Hinkel gave it a long look. "Carlo," he said. "One thing's for sure. You ain't never gonna need Viagra." I tried to hand the belt to him. "Uh, no," he said. "Keep it. At least 'til Friday. I got plenty more at home. I'm a dancer."

I bent over to pull my clothes out of the costume bag. Behind me, Hinkel was awfully quiet. When I stood up, he was turned the other way, getting into his underwear.

We asked Marlene if we could store our bags in the office. I handed her the bra. She held her hands up to ward me off. "No, you keep it. I'll take it back after work Friday."

The elevator was crammed with commuters, but Hinkel pushed his way in and pulled me after him. "How about we celebrate?" he suggested. "On me." I so wanted to celebrate on him.

We went to a dive bar in his neighborhood, Hell's Kitchen. "How can you afford to live in Manhattan?" I asked while we were waiting for our drinks.

Hinkel looked around. "I live with a couple of other dancers. Where do you live?" he asked, making my heart go pitty-pat.

"Queens."

"No shit. I'm from Queens. What neighborhood?"

"Long Island City."

"Not too long a subway ride," he said.

"Where in Queens are you from?" I asked. He was busy trying to tip the bartender and didn't answer the question. The guy just gave him a wink and pushed the money back at him across the bar. A table opened up; we made a rush for it.

"So, you're a dancer?" I asked after we sat down. "I've been thinking about taking dance lessons."

"You should. Can you sing?"

"Some. I was in a choir back home."

He looked at me with a grin. "Choir boy, huh? Anyway, that's the way to do it. Triple threat. Me, all I can do is dance." He didn't sound happy about it but, before I could say anything, he stood up abruptly. "I'll get us a second round." His ample crotch was in my face.

"It's my turn," I said to his crotch.

"Don't spend your money on me, Carlo. $500 won't last long."

"It's okay. I start a regular job next week."

Hinkel sat back down.

"Yeah? You in a show?"

"I wish. No, I'll be waiting tables at a new restaurant called McIver's."

"I heard about that place. They say it's gonna be really nice. Big spenders. You'll get some great tips." He leaned back in his chair. "I gotta get a job, too. I just quit one. Bike messenger." I thought about his big thighs pumping up and down all-around Manhattan, which gave me ideas, one of which wasn't sexual.

"McIver's is still hiring."

He settled all four of his chair legs back on the floor and scooted closer to me.

"Maybe we could go there tomorrow," he said, "after we hand out all the cards. That would be so cool, Carlo! Thanks!" His lips pursed or puckered; I wasn't sure which. He stood up before I could decide. "Now I gotta buy the next round."

On my way to the subway, I called my friend Debbie, who got me the job. "Describe him," she told me. "Hmm," she said after I did. "I think I've got something for him." Tuesday, mid-morning, Debbie called back.

When my mobile rang, Hinkel asked, "That you?"

"Yeah," I said, pulling the phone out of my crotch.

"Damn, Carlo. I thought that was your dick again."

"Hi, Deb," I said into my phone, turning away so I could hear what she was saying. "Really? Oh, that's great! Thanks, Deb! You know it, girl. Bye."

I turned back around, smack into Hinkel's body. I ignored the feel of his crotch against mine. "We're on. 6 p.m. tomorrow. Do you know how to tend bar?"

"Not really, but I know a guy'll teach me. I've done him some favors."

The guy was the bartender at Hinkel's dive bar. He agreed to train him, which was great, but his hands were always touching Hinkel's body somewhere while he was showing him what to do—which was not great at all. When I left, Hinkel was still practicing and the bartender's hands were still feeling him up at every opportunity.

"That guy is coming on to you," I whispered when I said good night.

"Really?" Hinkel asked, all innocence.

Wednesday, Hinkel wore a hot outfit to work for the interview: a tight white dress shirt open a couple of buttons, tighter black slacks, and a black leather jacket.

"Do I look okay?" he asked, sounding nervous.

"You look amazing. I'd hire you." He looked a little tired, though. "How long did you practice after I left?"

"Couple hours," he answered, sounding evasive. "I think I memorized every fucking recipe in the book."

Just then, Marlene got off the elevator. "Wow, Hink! Smokin', babe!" she said as she came up with the key. Hinkel winked at her and at me. He was handsome enough to make people pay for it.

We finished at 4 and ran up Broadway to save time. Mr. Marx accused us of dumping cards so we could leave early. Hinkel accused him of trying to cheat us. Marlene played referee. We got our money and left.

Outside, on the street, Hinkel smelled his armpit. "Man, I'm ripe. I gotta take a shower."

"I'll meet you at McIver's then."

He raised my left arm. "You stink too, Carlo. We can shower at my place." That gave me most of the same ideas I'd had on Monday.

His apartment was a fourth-floor walk-up in a building that had seen better days a long time ago. None of Hinkel's roommates was home.

"Come on," he said, leading me down the hall. "We gotta hurry." He began pulling off clothes as soon as we got into his bedroom. I just stood there, frozen by the fact we were alone in an empty apartment next to a rumpled double bed. He yelled at me. "Get naked, Carlo! We gotta shower together."

I tore my clothes off as fast as I could. Hinkel strode across the hall to the bathroom and was standing in the shower stall with water running down his tan when I came in. My cock was at full vertical.

"Damn, Carlo," he said, pointing. "No time for that. Get in here!"

I crowded next to him in the narrow space, all body parts touching. He scrubbed me down before I could ask for the soap. I lost it then and there. Hinkel didn't seem to notice.

We dried ourselves quickly and headed back to the bedroom. I noticed more this time, like the colognes lined up on his dresser and the photo of a beautiful young woman.

"Pretty girl," I said, trying not to look at Hinkel's body. He had dropped his towel. "What's her name?"

"Joanie. Hey, help me pick something out. What I wore today stinks."

We looked in his closet and agreed on black. While we dressed, I asked, "How long have you been together?"

He buttoned the black dress shirt into place snugly around his torso and asked, "Huh?"

"You and Joanie."

"Jeez, Carlo. Joanie's my sister."

At McIver's, Debbie came out to meet us with a hug for me and a handshake for Hinkel. She looked him over and unbuttoned another button on his shirt. "There," she said. "That should do it."

Before he left, I straightened his collar and whispered, "You look wonderful."

He gave me a tense smile and whispered back, "Thanks, babe." I watched him walk away with Debbie, cherishing the *babe.*

When Debbie came back, she flopped beside me on the banquette. "Whoo baby! Where'd you find him?" I didn't want to tell her about the chicken gig, so I just smiled. "You two make a cute couple," she advised.

"We're not a couple. Hinkel's not gay."

"You sure about that? Anyway, too bad. I had my bud married. Is he single?"

I looked at her. "He's got a girlfriend."

"Damn."

We talked show biz for the rest of the thirty minutes we waited. Debbie was an aspiring electronic violinist. "How did you two meet?" she had asked again just when Hinkel reappeared with a big smile on his adorable face. I noticed his shirt was open several more buttons and was hanging out of his pants. He stuffed it back in while we watched him walk towards us.

"I think I got it, babe!" he said, grabbing me in a bear hug and lifting me off the ground. *Babe* again. I was so happy. Debbie interrupted my bliss.

"Okay, guys. I have other people to interview. Hinkel, I'll let you know what Stan says, but I'm pretty sure it'll be good news." Stan was the bar manager. I'd never met him. Debbie gave Hinkel a weird grin and a thumbs up.

That night, I got two calls. The first was from Hinkel before I got home.

"I got it, Carlo! Man, I wish you were here. We have to celebrate." I could hear background noise.

"Where are you?"

"At the bar."

I wondered if the bartender was feeling him up at that moment. Probably not. He wasn't breathing heavily or anything.

That's when the second call came in. "Oh, it's Debbie. I'll call you back." I clicked Hinkel off and Debbie on. "Hi, Deb. I was just on the line with Hinkel. He said…"

"That's what I want to talk to you about."

"I know Hinkel got the job. Thanks for helping him."

"He helped himself. I knew he was Stan's type."

"What's that supposed to mean?"

"Did Hinkel tell you about his interview?"

"Just that it went well. You were there."

"Carl, I like you. We're friends. Friends tell you what you need to hear. Remember that."

"Debbie, what are you trying to say?"

"What I'm saying is Hinkel got naked and blew Stan to get the job.

"Debbie, that is not funny." I hung up the phone and thought about going back to Michigan. Instead, I called Hinkel.

Before he said hello, I asked him, "Did you blow the bar manager to get the job at McIver's?"

"Carlo…"

"Did you?"

"Babe…"

"Just answer, Hinkel. It's easy. Yes or no."

"It's not easy, Carlo."

"Yes, or no?

"Yes. You happy?"

"And how *do* you afford an apartment in Manhattan? Got a deal with the landlord too?"

"Look, we can talk about it tomorrow, after we hand out the cards."

"I won't be there," I said and hung up. I fumed for a while, then felt guilty. I almost called Hinkel back, but couldn't think of what to say. I wasn't sorry. What did I have to be sorry about?

Early the next morning, our doorbell rang. I leaned out the window. There was a six-foot-tall rooster on the stoop of my building. "I don't want to talk to you," I yelled down.

"You're gonna anyway," the rooster said. "Now, let me in or I'll keep ringing. You got roommates?"

"I'll come down."

I opened the inner door, and Hinkel muscled inside the foyer. "Which floor?"

"The second."

He started walking toward the stairs.

"At least take that stupid rooster head off!" I yelled after him.

"I'll take the whole damn thing off," he said and started stripping before he reached the second-floor landing.

"Okay, okay. Keep your britches on." Neither of us laughed.

I hurried past him and opened the door. Hinkel looked around my apartment. "You live alone?"

"My roommate isn't awake yet. I hope." He worked nights. I wondered what he'd think about a hot, half-naked man sitting on our couch, which is where Hinkel had plopped himself. Not much, probably. Both of us were gay; it had happened before.

"Sit," he commanded, patting the sofa next to him.

"Let's go in the kitchen."

I sat on a beat-up dinette chair. I'd found two on the street. Hinkel took a breath and began. "First off, you're right. I'm a whore, but it pays the bills. Second thing, why are you so mad?"

"Why wouldn't I be mad? You lied to me."

"I did not. I do have a great deal on the apartment, and I did get the job."

"But you blew Stan. And I don't know what you did to get the apartment."

"I fuck the owner once a month. There. You happy?" Hinkel crossed his arms and spread his legs, which was doubly distracting for me. He noticed. "I could fuck you," he said. "Would that make it better?"

"No!" I answered, less than resolutely. I got up quickly. "I think you better leave."

Hinkel stared at my crotch, which was letting me down again, then up at my five-alarm fire face.

"Isn't that what you really want? I seen how you look at me." I looked away. "It's okay, babe," he said. He scooted closer and tried to put his arms around me. I wanted to resist, but I loved it too much. I loved his hands pulling my shirt up and attaching themselves to my chest. I loved….

I pushed him away. "Hinkel, no." He held on to my ass.

"Babe, I really do wanna fuck you," he said. His icy eyes looked up at me sincerely. His brow was wrinkled with hope. "All week I been staring at those tits and this ass." I didn't bother reminding him the tits were socks. Besides, he was manhandling the real ones now.

"Uh, okay," I said.

"Where's the bedroom?" he whispered. I detached myself from him and led the way.

"I say we get naked," he said with a grin once we were in the bedroom. He began discarding clothing left and right. I hurried to catch up, but he still helped me before I finished.

In one slow movement, he lowered us onto the bed. I soon found out why he landed the bartender's job and how he got the apartment.

After he finished, he got back into his rooster outfit. "Time to go." He pulled the hen's costume out of the bag and stuffed me into it. We headed out for the subway. I didn't care if people stared. Hinkel was my rooster, and I was his hen.

***

He slept over, maybe to make sure I showed up for our last day. It didn't matter why to me; he made it worth it. We rode the subway in human clothing the next morning, with our costumes in his backpack.

"Come on," he said outside Marx Novelty Acts. "Let's do this thing one more time." We said hello to Marlene, and I followed him into Mr. Marx's office. We dressed in silence and set out for our now familiar spot in Times Square. The free chicken certificates flew out of our bags. At four p.m., we trudged back up Broadway. Marlene was leaning on the doorjamb.

"Yay, chickens! Mr. Marx had to leave. Don't worry. I've got your money." She waggled a wad of bills at us.

Hinkel muttered, "Thanks," brushed past her, and headed into the inner office.

"What's up with him?" Marlene asked. "Anyway, here." She handed me the money.

"Thanks, Marlene. I'm… I'm…"

"Me too, Carlo." She patted my shoulder. "Maybe you'll have another gig with us. Now, get out of that outfit. I'd like to leave a little early too." As I walked into Mr. Marx's office, she called out, "And don't forget my bra!"

Hinkel was already dressed. I counted out five twenties and handed them to him. "You keep it," he said. "You earned it. How's it feel to be a whore?"

"Hinkel!"

"It's Joseph. See ya around." He hefted his backpack and started to leave.

"Wait!"

He stopped but only half turned around. "What?" he asked. His blue eyes were shooting bullets at me.

"Look, I'm sorry I said anything."

"No, you're right. I'm a whore. You on days or nights at McIver's?" That gave me some hope.

"Days."

"Too bad," he said, sounding almost believable. "I'm on nights."

I grabbed his arm. "What are you doing this weekend?"

He stared at my hand until I let go. "Oh, let's see. Well, Saturday I'm fucking my landlord and Sunday Stan is giving me some special training. Looks like I'm booked." I took both slaps like I deserved them. The steel in his eyes melted. "Hey, babe," he said softly, his long, slender fingers lifting my drooping chin. "I'm free tonight."

In the middle of our moment, Marlene spoke up. I'd forgotten she was there. "Are you guys done? I'm going to miss my bus."

"Oh, sorry!" I pulled the spandex over my head. Hinkel undid the bra and returned it to its owner.

"I'll never wash it again!" she declared, with much batting of her Lilly lashes. She gave the bra a sniff before putting it in her gigantic purse/bag, then started tapping her foot. With Hinkel's help, I exited the rest of my clothes super fast. He folded and stashed the hen outfit in his backpack while I rushed into my civilian clothes.

"Who knows? We might need it again," he explained, and gave me a wink.

"Bye, Marlene!" we chimed as we left the MNA office at five till five.

"See you next time, boys!"

He and I walked to the elevator. I asked him, "Were you serious about tonight?" He stopped, clasped his arms across his chest, and asked, "Have you ever heard me tell a joke?"

I thought for a moment. "No."

"Well, then." He started walking again.

"Slowpokes!" Marlene yelled as she whizzed past us. She jabbed the elevator call button, and its doors magically opened. "Tah tah!" she yelled, waving at us as the doors closed.

Hinkel punched the button, then turned to me, bent his head, and gave me a lengthy kiss. "Might as well use the time," he said, pulling away to smile at me.

"Might as well," I agreed, pulling him back down.

The Green Bench

He was alone that morning, which disturbed me. Every day I walked through the park on my way to work and every day they were there, two old gentlemen sitting on the green bench side by side, sleeves touching, if not arms. In winter they wore overcoats, in spring windbreakers maybe, in summer short-sleeved shirts, and in autumn something heavier, a regular coat probably.

Today, it was just him, the One on the Left. He was slumping, but that wasn't unusual. He was quiet, but that wasn't out of place either. I hardly ever saw them speaking to one another. They just sat—wordless, motionless, but together.

I had never had the urge to stop, to know their names, but today, with the One on the Right missing, I felt the need to know why. Where was he? I looked at my phone; I would be late. I never gave myself more than the minimum amount of time to make the transit from home to office. A brisk walk was good for you, anyway. I sent a text to my secretary. I'd bring her coffee; she'd love me for it.

"Excuse me. You don't know me, but I was wondering, where's your friend?" No, I can't say that. Much too personal. Besides, is the One on the Right a friend or a lover? A brother? They do tend to dress something alike.

"Pardon me but my name is Paul Stallings and…." No, that won't do either.

"Excuse me. Is this seat taken?"

"No," the One on the Left said, looking up with sad eyes in a sadder face. He moved toward the left end of the bench. I sat near the right. There was still space for the One on the Right in between us. I hoped he was coming. I really hoped he was coming.

We were silent together, like they were. But silence wouldn't answer my questions.

"Lovely day."

"Yes," he answered, looking up and around. I looked where he looked. We wound up looking at each other.

"Would you like the *Times*?"

"No," he answered, trying to smile. "We… I have it at home." His face fell. He turned away from me, perhaps to hide his sudden emotion, perhaps to keep it private.

I hesitated. "Is anything wrong? Can I help you?"

He turned back to me. "I wish you could."

That seemed like an invitation to intimacy, so I moved closer, filling half the space we had left for the One on the Right. The One on the Left did not shift onto the other half.

"My name is Paul Stallings," I said, extending my hand.

He stared at it as if he were unfamiliar with the custom of shaking hands, but then, belatedly and in a rush, grabbed for it like he was drowning. "My name is Clayton Evers." We shook and then held hands as seconds ticked. Mr. Evers' hand was calloused and strong. If I'd only shaken hands with him, without seeing his face and body, I would have guessed he was much younger. When he let me go, I felt regretful.

He visibly pulled himself together and sat up straight, straighter than I'd seen him sit in three years of daily encounters, Monday through Friday only. "You're very kind," he said. I smiled. He took a breath.

"My partner died last night." That was as much as he could say. It seemed like a summary of much more.

I took his hand again and kept it. "I'm so, so sorry. It seems awfully sudden."

"It was," he agreed, then pulled his hand out of mine, looking at me quizzically—or suspiciously. I couldn't tell.

"I pass by here every day."

His expression remained wary.

"On my way to work."

He remained silent, leaning away from me, evaluating.

"I see you here every day when I pass."

He examined me more carefully, then seemed to relax. "Oh, yes. You're the Man Who Stares."

"What?"

"Bob and I noticed you always stare at us as you walk by. We called you the Man Who Stares. I'm sorry." He seemed embarrassed.

I tried to laugh, for his benefit. "I guess I did. I guess I was curious about the two of you. I mean, you're here every morning on the same bench, sitting beside each other, not saying anything."

Mr. Evers chuckled. "Well, we did talk *sometimes*, I'm sure, but after 43 years, you don't need a lot of words."

We sat silently on the green bench for a few moments. Mr. Evers looked at the duck pond. I looked at nothing. I began to think I should be saying goodbye.

"Bob was 81, eight years older than I."

I liked the attention to grammar. I hesitated, then took the plunge. "Mr. Evers, pardon me, but could I ask how your partner died?"

"Of course. And my name is Clay." I nodded. He sighed and said in a shaky voice, "It was a heart attack. He'd had two before, but recovered. This time...." His voice trailed off. I moved close beside him and put my arm around his shoulder. He leaned a little toward me. He probably did that with Bob.

"I'm sorry," he said. I could hear he was crying. Very quietly. I held him more tightly.

"There is nothing to be sorry about."

"Oh, but there is. In 43 years, you have plenty to be sorry about." His voice was rueful.

"But you were together all those years. You were in love." I was proud of myself for not stumbling over the word.

"Have you ever been in love?" he asked, looking askance at me but not pulling away. I shook my head no. "Well, I hope you find someone soon. When you do, you'll know what I'm saying."

"I can't see myself 43 years with anybody."

"Why not?" he asked, turning in my arm to look more directly at me.

Why had I made it about me? Jack said I always did that. I disagreed with him at the time, mainly because he was moving out and I was angry, but he was probably right. Looking back, he was right about most things we argued over.

"Oh, it's nothing."

"No, obviously, it *is* something."

He must be a kind man. Maybe it would help… no, no, no! "I'm just being silly. It must be terrible for you right now."

"I'm afraid it's going to be terrible forever," he said, trying to make a joke out of it. He looked at me again and caught me checking the time. "I'm keeping you."

He was. I needed to go on, walk away, be at work. It was Friday. So much to do. "Are you going to be here tomorrow?" I asked. He didn't look surprised, just said he would be. "I'll meet you here. What's a good time?" I wondered when he and Bob came to the green bench, when they left.

"We…." He stopped himself. "7:30 would be good."

"Okay, 7:30. See you then. Shall I bring you a coffee?"

"No, thanks. We always have… uh, yes. That would be great." I started to ask, but he answered before I could. "Regular, one sugar, please."

"Got it." I stood up, and Clay stood with me. We shook hands again. "See you tomorrow," I promised.

"See you tomorrow," he agreed.

The next morning, I made my way to the green bench, carefully carrying his regular and my black coffee. I let out my breath when I saw him sitting there in his usual spot.

"Good morning," I said to his back to let him know I was coming. He turned around, left arm resting along the top of the bench.

"Good morning, Paul." He had a lovely smile and a good profile. When I sat down beside him, I realized he was quite a good-looking man for his age. He must have been handsome when he was younger. What did—what had Bob looked like? Was he handsome, too? I'd really never seen his face.

"How are you doing today?" It was a pro forma ask, but I really did want to know.

"It's hard."

"Of course it is." I opened his coffee for him. He took several sips. "When is the funeral? You must have so much to do."

"Tomorrow. And no, I don't. Andrew, Bob's son, is taking care of everything, at least all that's left to take care of. Bob had already arranged most of it. He was a very organized person."

I tried to picture Bob. Clay seemed to be doing the same thing.

"Would you like to see a photo of him?" he asked. I said I would.

He took two out of his wallet. The first was of an elderly man with a wide smile and happy eyes. The second was of two men about my age, younger versions of Clay and Bob, I could tell. Clay was indeed very handsome, very blond, with regular features and a thick moustache. Bob was not so attractive, but he already had that wide smile and those happy eyes. He looked a little like me. I wondered if I should mention that to Clay.

"He had a great smile."

"He did," Clay said quietly. We stared at the photos for a while. I was beginning to get used to the silences. Clay looked up as if an idea had just occurred to him. "Would you come to his funeral?"

When I walked into Gershon's, the room was a sea of black suits and grey hair, with islands of blonde and brown. An usher handed me a program for the service. The room was nearly full. I hesitated, wondering where to sit, when suddenly Clay was in front of me, holding my forearm, welcoming me with words and smiles, and guiding me toward the front. He introduced me to Bob's children and then sat us down.

"I saved a place for you."

I should have said, "You shouldn't have," and retreated toward the anonymous back of the room, but I didn't.

"Thank you."

He linked his arm comfortably through mine. I saw Polly, Bob's daughter, notice. I wondered what I should do, but then the rabbi began, and we all faced forward. I hadn't known Bob was Jewish too.

After the rabbi finished, quite a lot of friends and family rose to tell stories about Bob. I felt I got to know him, know why Clay stayed with him for over 40 years. When Clay tried to speak, he broke down almost immediately. Polly was beside him in a second, taking his arm, whispering. Andrew and I sat marooned on the bench, separated by the spaces where they'd been.

Afterward, Polly spoke to me. "Thank you for coming."

"I'm Paul Stallings. I'm…."

"The Man Who Stares." She suppressed a smile. "Clay told us." She looked at me in an evaluating way. "You do look a lot like my father when he was younger," she decided, as if she were confirming information given to her by another source. "I heard you saying the Kaddish. Are you Jewish?"

Clay joined us before I could answer. "Thank you so much for coming, Paul," he said, taking my hands in his. "Would you like to join us for lunch?"

I made some excuse.

"Will I see you tomorrow at the green bench?" he asked in a voice full of hope and dread. Polly's eyes gave their approval. Something inside me did too.

"Of course," I assured him. "I'll bring the coffee."

Leprechaun in New York

He was a man hard to miss, even across a crowded room, with his skin like pink alabaster and hair like a torch. I had seen him several times before in this gay bar or that. He never went home with anyone, just drank and left. Tonight, I decided, he would go home with me. I caught his eye and set out on my quest but, when I reached the corner he always sat in, he was gone and someone else had appropriated his stool. I spun and caught sight of red hair moving toward the door. He was shorter than I thought. If he hadn't been ginger, I would have lost him.

Undaunted, I plowed through the mass of gay men celebrating St. Patrick's Day in the Hit and Run. I divided conversations like the Red Sea. When I finally made it to the door and outside, I just managed to see him turn the corner. On Twelfth, I saw neither hair nor skin of him but, in the one a.m. silence, I could hear the slap and splash of his boots as they hit puddles left by an earlier rain. I followed the sounds until he was back in sight, a half block ahead. I kept him in sight while keeping my distance.

A quarter block on, he turned into another bar, an Irish one I hadn't frequented since it was straight. The Dubliner was even more crowded than the Hit and Run, full of women as well as men celebrating St. Pat's in the traditional Irish-American way: with raucous laughter and too much alcohol. Sounds of *Slainte!* ricocheted across the room.

Only one in ten Irish person is redheaded, but all of them seemed to be in the Dubliner that night. I began a visual survey, although it was hard to see the trees for the forest. Happily, when my scan reached the bar, there he was, arms creating space on the dark oak, saucy ass firmly planted on a stool draped with his dark leather jacket. I squeezed my way next to him, made eye contact, and said *hey*. His pale eyes widened. Blue or grey, I couldn't tell. I could see though that he was as beautiful closeup as from afar—the fiery hair cut short but still curling back from an opalescent brow and down the temples, the wisp of a goatee accenting his blunt chin. His body was better too when it was next to mine—broad shoulders, a mounding chest apparent through a cranberry red shirt, muscled arms bulging in short sleeves. My fingers twitched in longing. I extended them to him.

"My name's Sean."

"Of course it is," he said with an undisguised sneer. After a moment's hesitation, he took my hand. "Aed."

"Ed?"

He rolled his eyes and looked around the room, as if to say, *can you believe this guy?* "No, *Aed*," he emphasized, dropping my hand. "It means fire." My eyes went automatically to his hair. He looked even more disgusted and started to depart for more intelligent climes.

"Let me buy you a beer," I said to the luxuriant waves down the back of his head. He turned around, wearing an unexpected smile.

"I'll take a Guinness, thanks."

I indicated to the bartender I'd like two pints of the dark stuff and, while it poured into the glasses, I tried to think of subjects to discuss that wouldn't drive him away.

"How long have you been in New York?" was my brilliant beginning.

"Oh, all my life," Aed answered in his deep brogue. He laughed in a high pitch. "Just three years. And you?"

"Oh, all my life," I repeated, telling the truth. "My grandfather came over after the war."

"Married a local lass?" I nodded. "Irish?" I nodded again. "We're both 100% then," he said with a look I couldn't interpret in the dark of the bar. Thankfully, the beers arrived sooner than expected and were gratefully received.

"*Slainte*," I said, clinking his Guinness against mine.

He took a long drink. "*Go raibh maith*!" he replied when he surfaced.

"What does that mean?

"Thank you," he answered before he took another long swallow, which drained nearly half the glass. He was ready for seconds when the bartender came by with one in his hand. He set it down in front of Aed. "They know me here," he explained. The sound of his thickening brogue sent shivers up my back and unsettled my groin.

He drank the second beer more slowly, maybe because I was still working on my first. I observed him intently, hoping I wasn't too obvious. Aed was no more than five-foot-two, but he was well and solidly built. He seemed to be assessing me as well. I prayed he liked five-foot-nine, dark hair, and a tidy beard. We drank our drinks and continued our evaluations.

When I asked him home, he gave me an excuse, drained the last of his fourth pint, repeated his thank you, and said "*Oiche mhaith,*" which I assumed meant *good night*. Or maybe *fuck you*. I didn't have my granny to ask anymore. Whatever the words meant, I was alone in a loud and happy crowd and wondering why. I chugged the rest of my beer and became his stalker once again. He was too handsome to let go, even if I wasn't his type.

He had another lead, and I let him keep it. He didn't walk far, just past Tompkins Square to a basement apartment on Avenue A. He trotted down a series of steps, opened a door, and closed it behind him, leaving me on my own again. *Now what*, I asked myself. *Oh well. At least I know where he lives.*

All through the week, I thought about the man with hair the color of fire. On the weekend, I walked by his building, hoping to see him. I did not. He wasn't at the Hit and Run or Dubliner either Friday or Saturday.

The next week I tried again, secluding myself in a doorway near his apartment early on a Monday. At 7:30 a.m. he hurried up the basement steps and trotted west. I trotted after, worried Aed would hear my labored breathing.

Between First and Second Avenues, he stopped in front of a shoe repair store and unlocked the door. He was a cobbler then. Didn't I have some shoes that needed mending? The next day I brought them to him.

"Well, hello!" I said, as if I were surprised. "Didn't know you worked here."

"Three years," was his curt reply. Daylight showed his eyes were pale green, almost translucent. He took the shoes, looked them over top, bottom, and sides, and asked, "New heels?" After I agreed, he wrote the receipt, put my shoes on a shelf, and turned back to his work. For too many minutes, I watched him remove old heels and soles and apply new ones on other people's shoes. I concentrated on the ginger waves across his bent head. He looked up once and smiled. I felt encouraged, even if the smile was just the slightest of slight but, when another customer entered the shop, I realized I was late for work. I ran for the subway full of optimism. We would meet again, and we would speak. Who knew what might happen?

On Friday, fifteen minutes before the shop closed, I arrived with my proof of purchase. "Just made it!" I said.

"Indeed," he acknowledged, looking up at the clock before turning to take my two pairs of shoes from a rack nearby. He set them on the counter. "That'll be forty and six," he said confidentially, hands gripping the counter, torso leaning toward me. His chest was apparent and invitational under the leather apron and deeply V-necked shirt.

"You remembered my shoes."

"I remembered you," he said, with a smile a little broader than the one four days before. I matched his angle over the counter. He didn't pull back and didn't stop smiling, but just then an even later arrival entered his shop, and he reached for a pair of tan high heels. The customer paid with her card and quickly left. I took out my own credit card, but Aed ignored it. He came around the counter, locked the door, and turned the sign to closed. My heart *thumpity-thumped*.

He turned and stepped close to me. His mouth and body were inches from mine. "Forty and six," he repeated in a throaty whisper.

"Can I buy you dinner?" I blurted.

He smiled with lovely small teeth. "Surely, but first the forty and six." I extended my card, and he let our fingers touch as he took it. Spontaneous combustion! I watched him tap the plastic on a reader. The act made me shiver with anticipatory delight.

"Do I need to sign?" He shook his head no and returned my card. "Where shall we go?" I asked while he removed his tan apron. My eyes focused on the bulge in the crotch of his jeans and the tight orange of his shirt, an orange to match his hair.

"McNally's might be the place," he answered as he faced away from me and hung the apron on a peg, which gave me a good view of his excellent posterior. I knew McNally's, an Irish pub, not too far. I settled in to wait, and his look became suspicious. "I've a deposit to make first. I'll see you there, say 7:45?" Any dreams about sex among the shoes dissipated like smoke.

"All right then," I replied. He opened the door for me, and I created a close encounter, which confirmed Aed's interest in me or, at least, his body's. I took heart.

I arrived at McNally's at 7:30, wearing tight black clothing, my queer color of choice. 7:45 came, then eight o'clock, 8:15. By 8:30, even I had to assume Aed had stood me up. I swallowed the remains of my second beer and signaled for the check. I'd have takeout from the Chinese place on my block. Just then, Aed came in the door. His sullen eyes caught mine immediately.

Maeve, the cocktail server, arrived with my check. "Oh, is that the one you're waiting for?" she asked. Maeve and I stood, waiting for Aed to make his deliberate way to us. When he arrived, she handed him my check. "Aed, what were you thinking? This man's been waiting over an hour!" They glared at one another. When she folded her arms across her chest, he grudgingly fished out his wallet. Maeve left to ring up the charge. I continued to debate whether to stay or go, but Aed sat down. So, so did I.

I folded my arms across my chest. It had worked for the server. "What happened?" I asked.

He sighed and looked away. "I almost didn't come, but I figured you'd be after me whether I did or didn't." He didn't laugh, and neither did I.

Maeve returned with Aed's credit card receipt. "Patricia has a table ready for you," she mentioned as she slapped the faux black leather down in front of him. He bent his head over his calculations, signed, and handed it back. She looked at his math, said something in Irish, then in English added sarcastically, "Very generous, Aed."

The hostess appeared immediately thereafter and directed herself first to Aed—"Hello, Aed"—and then to me, "Your table's ready, sir." She turned and set out through the crowd without a look back. I followed as best I could. Aed trailed after us both. I glanced over my shoulder several times to make sure he was coming.

"The special's steak and kidney pie. You'll be having that, Aed?" Patricia asked in her own Irish accent. He nodded his assent. She handed me a menu clad in more faux black leather. I handed it back.

"Fish and chips, please."

"Guinness all around?" she asked. Aed and I nodded in unison.

While we waited for our beers to dribble out, Aed made guesses about my Irish ancestry, my livelihood, and how old I was. "You're Black Irish," he said. My dark hair, pale skin, and deep blue eyes make that an easy assumption. And then there's the last name.

"Quaid, is it?" he guessed correctly. He didn't volunteer his. He went on to guess I was in banking and twenty-five years old. He was right on both counts.

"How did you do that?"

"Magic," he disclosed succinctly. Silence ensued.

I broke it by asking, "And what's your last name?" Maeve arrived at that moment with our beers.

"O Cleirigh," he answered, bending his head back to take a deep drink of the brew.

"He spells that different from what you'd think. The old way, is it, Aed? I'm a Donohue myself." She looked from one to the other of us. When there was no response, she said brightly, "Well then. *Slainte!*" and whisked herself away. Aed muttered something under his breath.

"What was that?"

"Nothing. *Slainte.*" He held his glass in the vicinity of mine without clinking, and we busied ourselves with our drinks for a few minutes. Aed had a second in short order while I nursed my third. The few questions I asked were met with suspicious looks and cryptic responses. Blessedly, a young man arrived with our food before our conversation completely stalled. I'd eat, pay the bill, and go. As I sawed into my battered haddock, I made a final, lame attempt at breaking through.

"How's the steak and kidney pie?"

Aed drained his glass. "Just like mam used to make." He held up his glass. Maeve was already on her way with its replacement. "Come now, lad. Have another," Aed said almost convivially.

I nodded a reluctant yes up at the server. After Maeve left, Aed reached a pink hand across the table. "You know, you're a mighty good-looking fella." Another surprise. Alcohol seemed to have worked the trick. Maybe stalking wasn't such a bad idea after all.

Conversation began to flow as freely as the beer. Aed told a story about Mongan, the great Irish mythological hero. "And a great hairy beast, he was, I can you," he declared as if he'd been on the scene of Mongan's adventures. I loved the cadence of his voice. Irish may not be the loveliest language, but Irish-accented English is musical. During the story, Aed shifted his chair closer to mine and drank his fourth beer. Over the fifth, he began to sing songs from the old country—and I'm not talking 'Danny Boy.' At the downing of his ninety-sixth ounce, Aed's arm went around my shoulder and his face peered into mine. "Shall we go to your place?" he asked. I nodded groggily, and he called out loudly in Irish. It must have been about settling up because Patricia arrived with the bill and an admonition to speak more softly. Aed paid without a grumble. "Come on then," he said and pulled me up from my chair like a one-handed deadlift.

He held onto my hand as we threaded our way through McNally's and out the door and didn't drop it all the way to my apartment in a high-rise at Fourteenth and Second. Getting there, we bumped into one another more than once. I laughed hysterically each time. Aed merely chuckled in a deeper register. His eyes had a determined glint.

At the door to my building, he slid a small hand into my back right pocket and squeezed my ass while I tried to match the key to the foyer lock. My motor skills were off. The hand in the pocket spurred me to greater effort, however, and I succeeded in opening the door the next try and ushered him in with a sweep of my arm. I kept the door open by leaning across the bar. I nearly fell, but Aed caught me.

"Come on, boyo. I got ya." We staggered together toward the elevator. Inside it, he watched me punch the button to seventeen. "Sure, and you've a terrible lot of floors in this building." As the elevator rose, he seemed to become even paler—if that was possible.

Aed rushed out when the elevator doors opened at my floor. I stumbled after him and led the way to number 1705. While my key fumbling had a reprise, he waited impatiently, tapping the toe of one highly buffed boot on the blue hall carpet. "Oh, here! Let me do it!" he declared, and grabbed my keys. He deftly inserted the correct ones into the lock and double lock. Inside, I took his jacket to hang and paused to admire how well his shoulders, chest, and arms filled out his red checked shirt. No wrinkles!

"You look good in red."

"Thanks, boyo. It's my favorite color." He looked over at the living room window. It was almost floor to ceiling. "Do you mind me closing those drapes? I'll be getting vertigo up here." The brogue was stronger now, and he spoke more Irish, most of which I didn't understand.

After shutting out the world, he turned to me and said, "*Tus maith leath na hoibre.*" I knew what that meant. It's an Irish saying. A good start is half the work. Well, I was ready for an overhaul. I collapsed onto the couch. Aed strode from the drapes to me, removing his clothing along the way. By the time he reached me, he was down to his underwear. His chest was a marvel—tight muscles the palest of pinks and lightly brushed with hair a darker red than crowned his cranium, each pec tipped by a cotton-candy pink nipple, perfect in circumference and diameter and ready to nibble on.

He busied himself with my garments, first the shirt, which he pulled off entirely and tossed haphazardly aside. I'm sure I saw buttons fly. He placed both of his hands firmly on my chest and gave each pec a squeeze, as if he were testing me for ripeness. I was ripe all right.

"Beautiful," he said, taking the words from my mouth—and speaking of my mouth—he began kissing it aggressively. His kisses were many and urgent and proceeded quickly down my neck and onto my chest. He pressed me downward. I stopped us at a 45-degree angle. Bottom wasn't my usual position, but Aed assumed hesitation equaled yes and flattened me against the cushions. He tucked his little fingers inside the hem of my briefs with a leer on his face. I started to say, "I'm a top," but that information was smothered by another flurry of Aed's kisses. *Oh well,* I thought, and made the best of it. I could run my fingers through his curly hair as much as I wanted, and each time he looked up, his eyes seemed greener and glossier. I cupped his face in my hands.

"What?"

"Such a lovely green."

"Really?" He sounded irritable, as if that were a bad sign. The hue of his eyes dimmed. I thought we were done for the night, but then he whispered, "I have condoms," and his eyes were bright green again.

"So do I," I whispered back, hoping at least to take a turn. He ignored my whisper and reached for his pants. I prepared myself by clenching my fists and gritting my teeth.

"Just relax," he said in a low throaty coo, which sounded familiar because I had said the same thing in the same voice to a sizeable number of men between my fourteenth and current year. I took a deep breath. In two minutes, the deed was done—maybe ninety seconds. I'm sure my neighbors enjoyed Aed's elongated groan and curses in Irish. He slumped against the couch. His handsome chest heaved with the record-setting effort.

"Ah, but it's been such a long time," he said, with what sounded like regret rather than pleasure. He looked askance at me. "I guess you'll be wanting your three wishes now."

I blinked. "What did you say?"

"Nothing," he muttered. "How about another go?"

"All right," I said. "But not here." I led us to the bedroom. Before we climbed onto the bed, I informed him, "I'm a top." He just chuckled and patted my back.

"Sure ya are."

Oh well, I thought, *at least it will be over quickly*. Of course, this time it wasn't. Aed performed like he had viewed an instructional video on the way to my bedroom. After the big finish, he exhaled dramatically. "Whew! You'll be making me weak at the knees, boyo. How about a cuppa?"

Over the tea, he asked if I'd been to Ireland.

"Yes, twice."

"Do you know much about the fairy stories?"

"Some," I said, remembering books my mother had read to me. "What should I know?"

"Nothing," he answered, gulped down the rest of his tea, and stood up in a lurch. "Well, I'd best be off."

"You're welcome to stay. I'll make us an Irish breakfast."

His suspicious look returned. "I suppose you have Lucky Charms and all."

"Well, yes, but I was thinking sausages and baked beans, tomatoes and..." He headed for the living room in the middle of my recitation of our possible menu. I followed, in time to watch him cover his body with clothes again in short order.

"What's wrong?"

"Nothing," he answered as he pulled on his beautiful boots. I knew now they added two inches to his height.

"I thought we were having a good time."

"We were," he confirmed, before retrieving his coat from the closet. Although he didn't ask for it, I gave him my deets and hoped for an exchange of social media—or at least a kiss. There was neither—just, as they say, an Irish goodbye. I watched the door close behind him.

Over the next twenty-four hours, I hoped Aed would call or text me. It didn't happen on either Saturday or Sunday. I waited a week without any word from the redheaded cobbler. At the beginning of the second week, I went by his shop with more shoes, but his hello was curt and my attempts at conversation were rebuffed. When I collected my mended soles and heels late on a Friday, he said a gruff "no" to drinks and dinner.

Still, I stayed home, hoping he'd text, call, or send me a message. When he didn't, but friends did, I grabbed my coat and walked out into the night before I could say no again. *Don't waste another weekend*, I advised myself.

Don and Dave were kind and comforting. We met in a bar, not the Hit and Run or the Dubliner. They asked how I was, and I said I was fine. The look they exchanged told me they heard the lie but had decided to ignore it. They bought me drinks and passed along funny gossip to cheer me up. Over the rim of the second pint, I saw Aed come through the door. I almost spilled my beer in the hurry to intercept him. My hand took hold of his shoulder, caressing it more than I meant to.

"Sean," he said, without turning to look. Eyes in the back of his head, this one.

"Can we talk?

"Sean…" he repeated with a deep sigh.

"Please, Aed. One more chance."

He turned at that and gave me a penetrating stare. The noise of the bar faded. I felt like we were the only two people in the world—just like in the movies. The focus of Aed's green eyes blurred, and something seemed to let go in his chest. His shoulders slumped. His head dropped. I was afraid he was fainting.

"What's wrong?" I asked, and put an arm around his shoulders to keep him upright. The color, such as it was for a redhead, came back in his face. He stared up at me with a lopsided grin and patted my hand.

"It's complicated, boyo. We should go to my place." My thoughts brightened and Aed chucked my chin. "Sure, and you're a handsome lad."

I waved goodbye to my friends as Aed led me to the door, his hand in mine. They waved back. I hoped they'd forgive me for deserting them. I'd call with an explanation—and details.

Aed and I walked along busy Saturday streets without words until Avenue A, where the thump of his boots and slap of my sneakers were audible in the quiet of the night. He looked at my feet. "You're not wearing your boots. And after all my hard work." He chuckled, but I didn't.

"Why have you been avoiding me? I'm sorry about the Lucky Charms—although I don't know why. Are you allergic?"

"Ah now, my treasure," he said and squeezed my hand. "As it happens, I like a bowl of Lucky Charms now and then. I'll be explaining it all once we're inside."

I waited two steps above him as he opened his door and flipped on the lights. His living room was unremarkably masculine--tan walls and plush darker carpeting, expensive looking brown leather chairs, a chocolate-colored sofa in more matte-finish leather, black and white photos across the walls.

"Do you want a beer?" he asked.

"No. I mean, no thanks."

"How about some whiskey, then? I have a bottle or two of Jameson's."

"I don't need a drink."

"Well, I do," he said with a grin. "Don't make a fella drink alone."

"All right then," I agreed reluctantly.

"What'll it be?"

"Jameson's please. On the rocks." *Just one*, I told myself. *I have to be clear-headed about this. Whatever this is.*

My brain may have been clear, but my eyes clouded with lust as Aed headed off for the kitchen. The view of his backside was too much to ignore. I was still a top, after all. When he looked over his shoulder, I quickly perused the photos. They were all by famous photographers like Diane Arbus, Annie Leibovitz, and Jay Maisel. There was even an Alfred Stieglitz. The newer ones were all signed.

I started to ask about them when he reappeared, but he handed me my tinkling, popping glass, tapped it with his, and said "*Firinne*. Truth," as a toast. The two words bothered me. I hadn't been lying, not exactly. My shoes really had needed mending. And for the rest, well… He downed his whiskey in a long gulp and poured another. I set mine on a cork coaster. Bad news is better heard sober.

"What did you want to say?" I asked.

He chugged his second three fingers and said in a rush, "I'm a leprechaun, Sean, and I'm really, really old."

"That's it. I'm done!" I jumped up. He pulled me back down. I resisted, but he won. I fell on top of him and he clamped his arms around me. I realized I was in my favored position at last, but it didn't seem an opportune moment to take advantage.

"Do you believe me?" he said up at me. His eyes were that emerald again.

"Oh, of course," I replied sarcastically. I was in the apartment of a crazy person. I needed to keep him talking while I figured out an escape plan. He brought us smoothly up to vertical. I bet he could lift twice his weight at the gym.

"Come now, boyo. Don't be that way."

I struggled in his grasp, and he let me go. "Okay, you're a leprechaun," I said. "Why tell me? Isn't that dangerous?"

"Yes, but I saw inside you." Images came to mind of organs, muscles, and blood vessels. "It's magic," he said. "The worst kind."

That gave me pause. "What kind is it?"

"Love," he answered with a downcast look.

"Oh," I said. I hadn't really heard him. I was busy thinking, *I will make a run for the door now*. He could have my coat, although it wouldn't fit him. I edged away a few inches. The glow in Aed's eyes faded, and his head dropped to his chest.

Against the advice of a saner angel, I asked, "What makes you think you're a leprechaun?" I vaguely remembered a list of delusions from college Psych 101. "Thinks he's a leprechaun" wasn't on it.

"I'm short with red hair and pink skin."

I nodded. It would be best to humor him until the right moment came to spring for the doorknob.

"My favorite color is red…"

I heard that and raised my hand. "Isn't it supposed to be green?

He waved my question away with a "totally incorrect" and went on with his list. "I live underground. I work as a cobbler. I have a…." I stopped him before he could finish.

"Check, check, check. But why does all of that make you a leprechaun?"

He looked at me like he couldn't tell whether I was putting him on. "Come with me," he commanded and yanked me up and after him down a hallway into his bedroom. He really was strong, which is something I usually consider a good thing in a man. I admit to having mixed feelings when I saw his extra-large and mighty comfortable looking bed. There would be plenty of room to roll around. I could pretend to show him some of my high school wrestling moves. Once I'd flattened him, who knows what might follow?

Aed pointed to the wall behind his bed. A rainbow arched above it, which I had to admit was surprising. He hadn't struck me as a rainbow and unicorns kind of guy, and it certainly didn't match the rest of the décor. With a different person, I might have questioned this perplexing lapse in taste, but with Aed I only shrugged.

"Good God, man, are you truly Irish?" He strode to the wall and took down a large photo of Ireland at one end of the rainbow, which revealed the door to a safe.

"Aed, you don't have to...." I stopped myself. I had no idea what he was doing, so how could I tell him not to do it? He twirled the dial right and left and right again, stopping at numbers along the way, then used a key to open the twelve-inch square door. I saw papers, boxes, and a bag inside. Aed removed the bag and rained its contents onto the bed. Gold coins, lots of them.

I stared at the pile and then at him.

"Well?" he asked, with tight lips and waiting eyes.

"Isn't it supposed to be in a pot?"

He grabbed hold of me and tumbled us onto the bed. His kisses overpopulated my face and his happy laughter reverberated in my ears while his hands busied themselves at my clothes and his until they were piles on the floor. We did indeed roll around a lot, but I wound up on the bottom again. All the while, I felt his hoard pressing into my back, hard and cold.

"This is crazy," I said when we were done and panting.

"*Focail leat!*" he shouted at me and sat up.

"I don't know what that means, but what I mean is making love on all your money."

He snuggled against me once again. "Oh, this isn't all of it, not even a tithe. Most of it's in stocks and bonds. And this building."

I sat up now. "You own this building?"

"Surely."

"Then why do you live in the basement?"

"I told you. I'm a leprechaun. Leprechauns live underground."

Hmm, I thought. Young man thinks he's an elderly leprechaun. Lives in the basement of the building he owns, rather than the penthouse. Has a rainbow above his bed and a sack of gold coins under lock and key. Likes Lucky Charms. On the other hand, he's handsome, hot, and fucks like a bunny. I told myself not to be picky. Dating a leprechaun cosplayer wouldn't be so bad—Aed wasn't green or anything—and, however old he imagined was, he was very very *very* well preserved. Besides, being in love with a leprechaun—which I realized I was—could hold all kinds of advantages, if he really was one.

"About those wishes…," I began.

"You only have three," he reminded me.

"No worries," I replied. "One is enough."

Heart Stealer

I DROVE FAST AND hard from New Orleans, where I live now, to Haney, Mississippi, where I was born and raised, to arrive as promised for Friday supper. I made sure to slow down to the posted twenty-five miles per hour through town. Haney had one policeman with not much to do. Once I reached the Carrie Anne Bar and Grill, which marked the town limits, I increased my speed through the woods.

The road was narrow and dark, but I knew the way and how fast to take the curves. But something unfamiliar made me ease my foot off the gas. Out of the corner of my eye, off to the right, I could see a light following me in the darkness. It dodged behind trees and leapt over bushes, keeping pace with my car. What could it be? My heart was beating like a drum at a New Orleans funeral.

When I reached the McCready soybean fields, the light disappeared. I admit to breathing a little easier until I looked back. The light was still there in the woods, like it was waiting for me.

At home, I parked the Charger in my folks' driveway, locked it—although nobody in Haney would steal anything anyway, and took a nervous sweep of the thicket of trees behind the house. No lights anywhere, except on my parents' porch. I still had goosebumps though. I pondered my memory until Dad stuck his head out the front door and, like when I was a kid, put the devils to rest.

"You coming in or not?" he asked in his jovial, Lions Club way. I waved and hefted my one bag. "Here, let me take that," he said, striding over to me with his bowlegs and strong arms. We tussled over it, but I won. Dad chuckled. "Still going to that health club, I see." I stopped myself from flexing my free arm and, instead, put it around his shoulders in a hug. He gave me a peck on the cheek. One of the joys of my twenty-six years is that my father has never stopped kissing me—quick as the kisses always were, even after I informed him I'm gay.

"Come on in the house now," he said, pulling away but holding on. "Like a mirror," he mused, more to himself than to me. "Yes, sir, like a mirror."

We went arm in arm into the house my grandfather built after the war, dodging the screen door and the non-ADA compliant threshold. "Maggie!" he yelled. "Look what the cat dragged in!" I stepped from behind him, set down my luggage, and embraced my mother. She was still slender after fifty-two years.

"Mary Ellen and the kids will be over tomorrow night for supper," she said into my ear, like it was a secret from Dad. "Oh, and Brewster, I suppose," she amended. The additional guest was Brewster Evans, my brother-in-law. He ran the gas station and auto repair in Haney. In the parlance, he was a good ol' boy. Therein lay the problem. My mother had married an attorney, and a mechanic was not a step up for her daughter.

She pushed me away. "All right, you two. John, you sit down. Rigby, go wash up. Supper is in ten minutes." I noticed my father head for the dining room. We'd be eating on the bone china and using the silver plate tonight, I guessed. Tomorrow, we'd probably be in the kitchen with the Corelle plates and flatware.

Over dessert—apple cobbler--I mentioned the light. "Must be the Heart Stealer," my father said, looking ready to say more. "Heard one was seen around here lately." My mother rolled her eyes, and I tried not to. Fortunately, my father didn't notice. He pushed back his chair, spread his legs, and settled his arms across his chest. Storytelling position.

He looked over his glasses at me. "Now, stop me if you've heard this one," he advised, just like he always did. "Yup, the Heart Stealer. Choctaw story, you know." He peered at me again. Dad's stories required audience participation. I nodded in confirmation, and he continued. "I forget the Choctaw name, but…"

"Hashok Okwa Huiga," I said. My parents looked at me like I was a talking dog. "I studied a little Choctaw history this year," I explained. "I mean, y'all keep saying we're native and all." My mother frowned. She is one-quarter Choctaw and takes that twenty-five percent very seriously. My dad is one-eighth, which makes me three sixteenths, an unsatisfactory fraction if there ever was one.

My father tried to repeat the Choctaw words. "Hayshook Okra Wayga." I did not correct him. "Anyway, this Hayshook travels at night and all you can see of him is his heart. That's the light you saw. Was it heart-shaped?" he asked. I shook my head no. Dad looked disappointed, but went on with his story. "Yup, I wager that was ol' Hayshook a-running alongside that souped-up car of yours, Rigby. Keeping up, I bet," he said with a question mark. I nodded yes. He looked gratified, then worried. "You didn't stare at the light, did you, son?" I admitted to some staring, and he gripped my arm, the strength of his fingers painful.

"Oh, no, boy! You daren't do that," he said with alarm. "That's how the Heart Stealer gets you. You stare at him, and you can't look away and, bam! There goes your heart!

My mother sat back against her Early American dining chair with perfect posture and hands folded in ladylike position on her lap. "And how exactly does he extract it, John?" My father raised his eyebrows at me, trying not to grin, and turned to her, as cool as sweet tea in mid-August.

"Well, now, Maggie. Some folks say he rips it clean out of your body"—he made a quick scoop at my chest with his left hand—"and others say it's more like a metaphor." He winked a *how's that* at me. I winked back *it was just fine*. "But how isn't material, Maggie," he said like the lawyer he is. "The point is, he's got it and you don't, and that's not good news for you." He leaned back in his chair again, looking mighty satisfied with himself.

My mother persisted though, as she is wont to do. "What does the Heart Stealer do with the hearts? My father looked flummoxed, so I changed the direction of the discussion.

"I've driven that same road at night and run through those woods plenty of times and never come across Hashok Okwa Huiga, not once."

"You were lucky," my father said. "Anyway, Hashok is a new resident, apparently. People only started calling 911 a couple weeks ago." He pronounced the Choctaw word correctly this time. With that, he slapped his thighs, stood up, and started clearing dishes. I rose to help him.

"Isn't there any more to the story, John?" my mother asked, remaining seating.

"Nope," my father answered with finality, taking dishes out of my hands. "You two go on into the family room. I know how to fill a dishwasher."

"You can't use the dishwasher, John, not with these dishes. You'll have to hand wash the silverware, too, please," Mother said quickly. "And leave those pots for me," she called after him as Dad bumped open the swinging door with his rear. It closed behind him without acknowledgment. "He always puts them back in the wrong places," she confided.

"I know," I said. I had a great personal fear of putting pots and pans back in the wrong places at my parents' house. I led us out of the dining room into the hall.

"He usually tells a story better than that," she said to my back. I made a note to do some more research and relay any information I found to my father.

"I see you bought a bigger screen tv," I remarked as Mother and I settled onto the divan in the family room.

"Yes," she said with a sigh. "Your father wants the television large enough so he can see the Ol' Miss players sweat. But the color is much better."

"You say that every time," I kidded. She shoved me gently with the flat of her right hand.

"Oh, Rigby, I never say any such a thing!"

She smoothed pink slacks I didn't remember.

"Are those new?" I asked.

She looked at her legs. "Yes, I bought them online."

"No!" I exclaimed. If my mother started buying her clothes online, Pretty Lady Boutique in downtown Haney was doomed.

"Don't worry," she said, as if she had read my mind. "I'll still buy plenty at Pretty Lady. They didn't have the right shade of pink." My mother is particular about her pinks. "It's flamingo," she added and looked at me like she was waiting for a response, probably because I'm gay and we all have excellent color sense, like all Black people can dance. Instead, I started an update about my life in New Orleans, but she interrupted with a dismissive wave of her hand. "Wait for your father," she said. "I want to hear more about this light you saw. It followed you, you say?"

"More like *accompanied* me," I corrected.

"Accompanied," my mother said thoughtfully, looking at the turned-off television for a few seconds. "What else happened?"

"Nothing. It disappeared once I got to the McCready soybeans."

"Did you look back?" she asked.

"Yes," I said. "I did."

"And?"

"It was still there in the woods," I replied, shivering a little. Mother looked like she was about to charge off to see for herself and give Hayshok what for. Chase my son, will you? "Probably just someone with a flashlight," I said, which did not account for the light keeping up with a speeding car. She usually isn't easily put off but, after giving me a disbelieving arch of an eyebrow, she was willing to change the subject.

"You still not seeing anybody?" she asked.

My mother has two grandchildren but holds out hopes for more. Admittedly, those hopes waned when I told her I was gay, but they came back strong after she saw a segment on PBS about Queer parents adopting or having children of their own. "You could get a surrogate," she informed me on my next trip home to Haney. I was still living in Belle Reve with David Lee at that time.

"No," I said, in reply to her original question, trying to keep it short.

"Have you tried online? I hear OkCupid works pretty well."

I did not want to get into OkCupid, much less Grinder, with my mother, but I could see I'd have to give her something.

"I have been on a couple of dates," I admitted. If she'd been a dog, her ears would have perked up.

"Now, that's interesting. Anyone nice?"

Two out of three were, in fact, nice and one was so handsome he made me nervous, but no bells rang. No bells had rung since David Lee. I shook my head more sadly than I meant to.

Mother's inquisitional look softened. "Now, honey, you can't grieve over that boy forever." She reached for my hand. I let her hold it but hardened my heart. I wasn't grieving, certainly not over David Lee Rutherford. All that stopped when I found out whom he was sleeping with while he was still wearing my ring.

About that time, Dad ambled into the family room, plopped onto his recliner, and hit the down button. As he descended to the perfect 45 degrees, he said, "Now, tell us all the news from the big, bad place you live in."

***

I slept well and got up early to go fishing. The night before, I asked Dad to join me, but he shook his head woefully. "Wish I could, son, but your mother has a quite a honey-do list for me. Can't get much done on it during the week." My father might be a country lawyer, but his business is steady.

I took the long trail through the pines to avoid alerting the McCready hounds. If they started baying, the whole county would be awake earlier on a Saturday than they wanted to.

At the creek, I could see someone had beaten me to my spot. He had his back to me, his bare back. It was broad and muscular and looked smooth, like my hand could run down it and it would feel like silk. Otherwise, he was in the good ol' boy uniform: scuffed boots, faded blue jeans, and a camo baseball cap.

I thought he must have excellent hearing because he turned to face me before I got within thirty feet. My mouth popped open like I was catching flies. My Lord! His chest! The man chuckled like he'd seen it before and had the sense to take it as a compliment. I blushed deeply red, muttered "Excuse me," and started to move further down the bank.

"Both of us can fish here," he said, stopping me in my tracks. His voice was deep and reverberating, like the beating of a bass drum.

I turned around and returned his smile. I couldn't tell much else about his face since his cap was pulled way down on his forehead, but men with bodies like his don't have to be pretty. He did have a dimpled chin and full lips, which took him far, I'm sure, but his chest remained distracting and disconcerting. I looked away, even though I didn't want to. When I dared look back, the stranger was pulling on a white t-shirt. I admit to being both relieved and disappointed. When his head popped through, he turned out to have dark curly hair, a boyish face, and large pale blue eyes. They flashed at me like headlights in the dark.

I began to consider the advisability of staying. This stranger made me nervous in several ways. For one, a man built like this guy could pulverize me if he had a mind to and for another those eyes, but he put his hat back on low and reached out a big paw, forestalling any immediate escape.

"Enoch," he said in his low, rumbling voice.

"Rigby," I answered, sounding a mite squeaky.

"Interesting name," he noted, cocking his head to one side—most attractively, I might say. He observed me for quite a while. At least, it seemed like quite a while. The effect of his eyes was muted by the shade of the cap's brim, but they still held me fast until they glanced down at his hand. I belatedly took it, and a jolt shot up my arm into my chest. Enoch smiled like he knew something more about me now. I snatched my hand away and busied myself baiting a hook. He took up his own rod and began fiddling with it. I tried to ignore him.

"I see you like crank," he said to my silence. "I favor jigs myself." There was no way around it; he meant for us to have a conversation. A thorough discussion of how and when and with what to catch bass ensued and, by the time we'd exhausted that subject, I had relaxed in Enoch's presence, although I did strive not to look at him below neck level. The white t-shirt served to cover his torso but didn't accomplish much about hiding it.

During a conversational lull, I cast my line into the water. Enoch cast his too, much further out. With arms like his, he could probably have snagged a tree on the opposite bank if he'd wanted to. No matter how many decades I went to the gym, I would never have guns like his. I felt envious and attracted at the same time.

"You live around here?" he asked casually, turning the handle of his reel but not his head. I knew what he was getting at.

"Used to," I answered. "I'm visiting my folks." I pointed vaguely behind me.

"Oh, you the one in that red Charger?"

"Good guess!"

"Saw it parked on my way here. That your folks' place?"

"Yes," I answered truthfully, wondering whether I should have. He asked where I lived now and I felt it was only polite to respond and then he asked another question and another and, before I knew it, the sun was climbing the sky above us.

"I better head back," I said, thinking of breakfast and my mother's preference for promptness. Neither of us had caught a thing, which was strange. I always caught something. I wondered if I should invite Enoch to breakfast, but that would only encourage romantic speculation on my parents' part, so I decided against it.

In the face of my announcement, he said with a sexy half grin, "I'm gonna fish a while longer here," like I'd said the considered invitation out loud. "But how about I treat you to dinner?" he suggested, meaning the midday meal. "You know of a good place? I'm pretty new in town."

"Irene's is good," I said, without hesitation beforehand and only a little regret afterward, thinking of my mother's delicious chicken salad sandwiches, my favorite, which she always served when I was home. When, and if, my parents met Enoch, they'd understand. Mother would say he was quite a catch, depending on what he did for a living. “On Front Street, just up from the Walgreens? I could drive us,” I said.

“You’re so sweet,” he whispered and leaned in, face approaching fast, eyes on high beam. One hand hovered over the center of my chest. As his lips landed against mine, his hand touched down as well. I felt a pleasant hum. When he pulled away, I was left a little breathless.

“Don’t know what time I’ll finish here,” he said, looking mighty self-satisfied for some reason. “I’ll meet you there. Twelve okay?” I nodded dumbly. He gave me a full-wattage smile and bent over to gather his pole and tackle box. That disclosed the waistband of his briefs, startlingly white against the deep gold of his skin. He straightened up, smiled knowingly, and loped off into the woods. After he disappeared, I walked haphazardly back to my parents, bumping into loblolly pines and accidentally scraping through brush along the way.

“You got a date?” my father questioned ecstatically, after I told my parents I wouldn’t be joining them for lunch. “In Haney? Who is he? Do we know him? What’s he do?”

“Now, John, leave the boy alone. It’s just a meal,” my mother said, with a look that telegraphed we’d talk later.

“Where y’all planning to eat?” my father asked.

“I thought we’d go to Irene’s,” I replied, hoping they wouldn’t read anything into my choice of restaurants.

“Better wear something nice,” my father advised. Irene’s sufficed for elegant dining around metropolitan Haney.

“And remember your sister’s coming over for supper,” my mother prompted, as if my lunch with Enoch might last more than six hours.

***

Outside Irene's, I looked over the row of parked vehicles, wondering which was his. Probably one of the trucks. He had that look. About then, I heard a tapping behind me. Enoch was knocking on the windowpane from the booth just inside, a different cap pulled low over his eyes. The baseball cap at the fishing hole was ratty. This one passed for good ol' boy formal: dark blue and no insignia. It might even be new. I'd have to check for a tag.

I joined him inside, waving at Joanne, the hostess, Millie the waitress, and Andrés, the cook. I found Enoch without Joanne's help and Millie sauntered over, sans menu. "The usual, Rigby?" she asked, and I nodded. "Glad to see you," she said. "You here visiting your folks?" I nodded again. "What's your friend going to have?" she asked, like Enoch couldn't order for himself. He was hunched over, eyes on his menu.

"What's good?" he asked me, ignoring Millie.

"Everything!" Millie declared. She peered at Enoch, angling her head this way and that. He resolutely kept his head down, studying his menu.

"Are you a meat eater?" I asked him.

"Surely looks like one to me," Millie said, with a hand on her hip. Her eyes trailed down his body. His white dress shirt was open two buttons, but you didn't need that to see what was inside. "At least, as far as I can tell with that hat on."

"I'll have a roast beef sandwich," Enoch decided, closing the menu with a slap. He looked up at me briefly. A flash of blue sent a thrill up my body.

"Cheese on that?" Millie asked, his hat brim.

"American, please."

"Fries or salad?"

"Fries, please."

"Anything to drink?" Millie asked finally, looking around the restaurant, ready to go.

"Coffee, please," Enoch answered, pushing his cap up slightly, but Millie had stopped looking. She snatched up his menu and briskly walked away.

With her gone, Enoch sat up straighter and pushed back his cap some more. His dark curly hair sprang into view.

"You look nice," he said. I had dressed in my Sunday go to meeting shirt, the same shade of pink as my mother's slacks. What dress shirt I'd wear tomorrow at church, I wasn't sure. Probably one of my father's.

"So do you," I allowed myself to say. I didn't want to get too effusive in public. Haney had quite an effective informal messaging system. Besides, I needed to ask some questions. My parents would require more information the next time I saw them, I was sure.

I cleared my throat. "What do you do?" I asked.

He looked surprised but replied concisely, "Construction. How about you?" I told him I was a lawyer. "That right?" he declared, like he was proud of me. His boot found my shoe under the table and stayed there. No jolt appeared through the leather. Thank you, Jesus.

"Whereabouts do you live?" I asked, trying to sound nonchalant, like uber attractive men put their tootsies on mine every day of the week.

"Off the main road, in the woods along Beaver Creek. Just before it joins the Pearl," he explained. My arms got goosebumps again.

"Say," I began, still striving for nonchalance. "Have you seen a strange light in the woods around there?"

"A light?" he echoed. "What kind of light?"

Enoch's face reminded me now of a witness who is not telling the truth, the whole truth, and nothing but the truth. I leaned across the table, observing. He removed his boot from my shoe.

We stared at one another without resolution until Millie's voice intervened. "Here y'all go," she said, setting his coffee and my sweet tea on the table between us. Truth be told, the interruption wasn't welcome. I was enjoying my observation of Enoch. I hadn't noticed before how high his cheekbones were. He must have Native blood too. I wondered if he were Choctaw, like three-sixteenths of me.

Millie left again, and I asked the next question on my mental list. "Where are you from?"

Enoch shifted uncomfortably. "Up north," he answered vaguely, and started sipping his coffee. My question was obviously one too many. We concentrated on our drinks after that for what seemed like an hour.

"Which one is your truck?" I asked eventually, to get us going again.

Enoch sat up a little and ventured a smile. "What makes you think I drive a truck?" I gave him one raised eyebrow, inherited from my mother. "That blue Dodge down there," he answered, pointing. We both craned our necks. His was a 17, I estimated.

"Been in Haney long?" I asked. His smile disappeared again.

"Two weeks," he answered, returning to not looking at me. "I been working a job site in Bay Saint Louis and got tired of the Gulf. I like being out in the woods."

"Lots of woods up north," I noted dryly.

Enoch looked out the window, like we could see them from our booth.

With a bang, Millie slammed his plate down on the table, which made both of us flinch and look up. "Ah ha! The man does have a face," she said, handing Enoch his plate without looking at me. Millie appraised him for a few seconds, still retaining my plate. He held her gaze. "Must be a burden having eyes like that," she commented matter-of-factly before hers drifted down his body. She winked at me and set my plate down at last.

"Watch out, honey," she advised with a leer. "It's hot." I figured she didn't mean my food.

Enoch and I began eating, which gave him another reason not to answer any more questions. I kept trying, but all I got out of him was grunts. If this was a date, it sounded as if it were over.

When our plates were clean enough to put back on the shelves, we tussled over the check, which you'd think would require some verbal exchange. It did, but not much. Enoch won by nearly ripping the bill out of my hands. He paid at the register while I waited outside. Once again conversational, he walked me to the Charger. "How long you planning on staying?" he asked, trying to dazzle me with a toothy smile and a tingling hand on the small of my back.

"Only until tomorrow afternoon," I replied, trying to ignore how good his hand felt.

"Sure wish I could see you again," he opined, looking young and wistful.

I clicked my car door open. *He probably won't even be here the next time I come home*, I told myself, feeling relieved, like I'd taken a deep breath.

"What about this evening?" he asked, trying out seductive and sexy since young and wistful hadn't worked. I started to tell him about supper with my family, but he stopped me with both hands up in mock surrender. "I know, I know," he said. "Probably having a family meal. But how about after?" That suggestion let me know he wasn't interested in me for intellectual stimulation.

"I don't know," I answered, trying to stall. On the one hand, it was hard to say no to a body like Enoch's. On the other, he was a teensy bit too pushy. Okay, way too pushy. I used God as an excuse for my indecision.

"I have to go to church," I said.

Enoch crouched over, hands on his thighs, guffawing. "That's almost as bad as I have to wash my hair," he said, slapping his tight indigo jeans. Several women in window seats inside Irene's seemed to be enjoying the view of his rear.

"You obviously haven't met my mother," I said as seriously as I could.

"What time?" he asked, suddenly stern.

"Pardon?"

"What time do you go to church?" he asked, more specifically.

"10:30," I answered in zombie mode. His eyes were flashing semaphorically, and his crossed arms accented his astounding chest.

"Plenty of time," he decided. "Stay here," he commanded, pointing at the ground like I was his dog, and ran back into the restaurant. I stayed, ignoring inner advice to drive away fast.

When he trotted back out, he had a piece of paper and a pen in hand. "Here's a map," he said and drew one for me. "To my place," he added, in case his intention wasn't clear. Any no I might have said was cut short by the directions on his map.

"Is that the old Swaim place?" I asked. "I'm surprised it's still standing."

"I did have to do some repairs," he confided, leaning closer, eyeing my mouth. The ladies who lunch were definitely getting a good show now. I took a nervous step backward and landed with a thud against my car.

"I hope you fixed the roof," I said, trying to sound like my mother. "Rains a lot here."

"Yup. All patched up. Should get me through the fall." He handed me the map, and I took it. Or tried to. He didn't let go, just kept staring at me with those eyes. I started to sweat. "See you tonight," he half-whispered and maneuvered close again, his face peering into mine. I smelled a woodsy scent emanate from him. Was he wearing cologne? Did anyone naturally smell like cedar and pine?

It looked as if the ladies inside Irene's were texting their friends at this point. "I better go," I stammered and flung my car door open, giving Enoch a wallop--which didn't seem to faze him at all. I slid into my front seat and shut the door between us. He tapped on my window; I felt compelled to let it down.

"Yes or no?" he asked, hands on the window frame, long body bent over to show me his head.

"We'll have to see," I answered from the safety of my bucket seat. "What's your mobile?"

"Doesn't work too good out where I am. Just come," he said. "I'll be up."

I tried unsuccessfully not to nod, started the engine, put the Charger into reverse, and hit the gas harder than I meant to, almost ramming a late model Ford station wagon, probably Mr. Emmanuel Henderson's. I waved my apology and shifted into first.

When I looked back—which I should not have done, Enoch was standing on the sidewalk, legs splayed, hands on hips, chin out, looking like an advertisement for Bass Pro Shop. He waved at me, palm up, hand slowly twitching side to side. I gunned the car and roared down Front Street toward home, ignoring speed limits and bored policemen.

***

At supper, I had trouble concentrating. I saw Enoch in my father and especially in my brother-in-law, even though Brewster had put on a few pounds since his high school football days. I even saw Enoch's sandwich in the pot roast Mother had cooked up for us. And then, Dad would have to bring up the Heart Stealer.

"Rigby saw a spirit comin' home last night," he said to the kids, wiggling his eyebrows and fingers. Mother and Mary Ellen looked at each other.

"Now, John…" Mother began. Mary Ellen frowned.

He ignored them. "Do y'all know about the Heart Stealer?" he asked Brewster Junior and Elise. They shook their heads no, eyes wide and mouths gaping. He then repeated the story from last night, although he judiciously omitted the ripping the heart out of your chest part. The story ended as lamely as before. The kids immediately lost interest and turned to me.

"Do you have a girlfriend yet, Uncle Rigby?" Junior asked. He was eight and had two gfs, at last count. My sister and I had agreed to wait until he was 10 to disclose my orientation, unless he asked directly whether I liked boys or girls.

Mary Ellen stepped in before I had to lie. "Junior, eat your green beans."

"But does he?" my niece asked. She was six and more interrogatory.

Mary Ellen gave her daughter a Mr. Rogers answer. "Your Uncle Rigby will let us know when he has someone special. Won't you, Rigby?"

"I surely will," I replied, smiling at Elise. She smiled back and resumed the attack on her plate. Junior worked his way diligently through his vegetables.

After supper, Brewster Senior took the kids to the family room and, from the sound of it, selected some G rated entertainment for them. How many times can a body watch *Shrek II*? Mary Ellen joined me in ferrying Corelle ware, everyday glasses, and flatware to the dishwasher. I handwashed wooden utensils and pots and pans while she dried, stowing everything in cupboards and drawers one by one, secure in the knowledge our mother would approve of their whereabouts.

"*Are* you seeing anybody?" she asked while I scrubbed the roasting pan.

"What happened to Uncle Rigby will let us know?" I answered, bumping her with my hip.

"Ouch," she pretend-protested. "Fair enough," she said, putting four of the wooden salad bowls away.

I stopped soaping the roast pan. "Actually, I met a guy today in the woods..."

Mary Ellen let the rest of the bowls be. "In the woods? Really, Rigby. This is not New Orleans. You oughtn't to be..."

"He was fishing at the fishing hole," I interjected. I declined to state he had been shirtless. "We had lunch together at Irene's."

Mary Ellen took up the remaining three bowls. "What's his name?"

"Enoch..." My voice trailed off.

"Enoch what?" she said, jumping on the pause. She should have been the attorney, not I.

"I don't know," I admitted.

"Hmm," Mary Ellen said. I had heard that hmm before. In court. From a judge.

"What's he do for a living?" was her next question for the prosecution.

"Construction," I answered, following advice I always gave my clients: be brief and truthful.

"Doesn't sound like your type," she commented as she took the rinsed roast pan from me. "Must be *really* good looking." I tried to remain silent, knowing I had that right. "Let me guess," she said, still holding the pan. "Tall, blue eyes, and dark curly hair?" Sisters. They know us too well. "Will you see him next time you're home?"

"Actually, I'm seeing him tonight," I confessed. "After y'all leave." When had I decided that?

Mary Ellen pursed her lips. "Do we at least get dessert first?" But thereafter, her frown ascended into a smile. "Go for it,

Rigby," she said, with love in her voice. "Play safe though. Promise?"

I crossed my heart. "Always."

***

After dessert, hugs and kisses, and repeated goodbyes out the front door, I told my folks I was going out. They were back in the family room, Mother on the divan and Dad in his recliner. They managed to take their eyes off the big screen but didn't ask where or with whom. "Be sure to take your key," my father advised, winking. Mother reminded me we were going to church in the morning. I found my jacket in the hall closet, stowed a couple of condoms in the interior pocket, and poked my head into the family room again.

"Don't wait up," I said.

"We won't," my mother replied, not taking her eyes off NCIS this time.

Dad looked over his shoulder, grinned, and gave me a thumbs up.

Once in the car, I debated whether to start it. Oh, hell! I said and revved her up. *I can just drive around for a while*, I told myself. My folks won't know the difference. Within minutes, though, I found myself on the dirt track leading to what had been the Swaim place before they all gradually died. I could barely make out the way through the crowding trees and overhanging branches. Were the woods always this dark? When I reached the house, it was dark too.

I assumed I'd been stood up, which pissed me off after all that talk. I backed my car up to turn around. About that time,

I noticed a light in the darkness, off in the trees. It seemed to hover. I cut the engine.

"Enoch?" I called.

"Over here," his deep voice replied. It was coming from the direction of the light.

I climbed out of the Charger and walked across crunching twigs and small rocks but, as I approached, the glow receded into the darkness. "Come on, Enoch. Quit fooling around." The light stopped, deeper inside the woods. "Enoch?" I asked again.

"I'm here," he said, sounding eerily like Jimmy Stewart over the telephone in "The Philadelphia Story." The Voice of Doom. I declared I was going home, and the light moved toward me. I could make Enoch out now. He was naked and wasn't carrying any flashlight.

"My God!" I screamed and turned to run, but a strong and speedy hand on my shoulder held me in place.

"Please stay," he said softly. I hadn't heard that softness in anyone's voice in quite a while. I hesitated, but fear won out.

"I know who you are. You're Hayshok…"

He put a finger to my lips. "You've known all along, haven't you?" he asked in a playfully insinuating voice.

I answered "no" but even I didn't believe me. Besides, Enoch, Hayshok, whatever his name was, was done with talking. In the middle of my answer, he slammed his chest against mine and clamped his arms around me, clasping his fingers together like a vise at my back. I felt heat against my heart. A glow eked out between our bodies.

"What the hell's happening?" I shouted in a panicked voice. After a few seconds more, Enoch pulled away, letting me go. Whatever he was up to, it was done. His face was calm.

"I've given you my heart," he said. I looked down at my jacket. The light in his chest had been transferred to mine. His chest was dark.

"I thought you were supposed to take them, not give yours away."

He chuckled. "You don't believe that old wives' tale, do you?"

"You're here, aren't you?"

He shrugged his wide shoulders and allowed that, "Some parts of the story are true." Then, he smiled and opened his arms for another embrace. I held him off with the flat of my hands.

"Wait a minute! Will I always glow like this?"

His huge laugh rang in my ears and throughout the woods around us. "No, *chukvsh champuli.*"

"What does that mean?"

"Sweetheart," he answered, and took me in his arms.

"When?" I insisted, trying without success to fend him off.

"Soon, I hope." And then he held me for a moment--tight but not crushing. When he released me, the glow was back in his chest. I didn't need to ask him what that meant. No, I asked myself, *How am I going to explain this to Mother?*

From The Sea

I KNEW JEREMY COGGINS came from money the first time I saw his car. It was a Maserati convertible, deep blue, and illegally parked outside Roble Hall at Stanford. I was admiring its just-waxed sheen when a voice behind me asked, "Need a lift?" My attention shifted from car to man. Seaweed green eyes and a flashy white smile, abundant hair the color of sand, and clothes I knew didn't come from Marshall's.

"No, thanks."

He leaned toward me, as if for a handshake or perhaps a kiss. "Jeremy Coggins."

"Andy Hawthorne," I said, prepared for either.

His forward progress halted. "Did you say Hawthorne?" Here we go.

"Are you related to…?"

"Yes," I said, too curtly, I'm sure, but I get so tired of answering the same questions. I wish I had more to tell. Yes, Nathaniel Hawthorne was my great-great-great-great-granduncle, but our family hasn't lived in the House of Seven Gables since his generation and any literary genius in us died out long ago. I wondered whether this Jeremy Coggins was an English major. They're the worst.

But instead of a literary interrogation, he followed up with, "My family's from Boston. Well, we were a long time ago. Gold Rush days. Do you like trees?"

I tried not to look too taken aback and answered, "They make fine furniture." He roared a great laugh and punched my shoulder.

"I'm very interested in trees."

"Is there a forestry major at Stanford?"

"I wish," he answered irritably. Then, with smile returned to full wattage, he asked, "Do you have any classes this afternoon?" I admitted I did. "Can you ditch?" he asked, his eyes excited. "We could take a run to Yosemite or Big Trees. Maybe both, if you don't mind staying overnight," he added. I looked him up and down.

After careful consideration of what he was offering—which was considerable—I said a reluctant "No."

"You're a serious student, then?" he asked without any detectable sarcasm.

"Very serious."

"Well, maybe another time." He looked up at the dorm. "Hey, do you live in Roble?"

"Yes, on the second floor. I'm a freshman."

"Me too. I'm on three." A pause ensued. "Right. Uh, well, I gotta go park this thing." He indicated the Maserati. He hopped in the car and waved with a jaunty flare.

***

The next afternoon, I was at my desk, seriously studying, when my door creaked open. It was Jeremy. "Andy, my man!" he exclaimed, and flopped onto my roommate's bed. His white shorts rode up, exposing muscular thighs and a startling tan line. "Do you play tennis?" he asked. I noticed a tennis bag by the door.

I produced my Babolat from the clothes closet.

"Excellent!" he declared. "Let's play. Do you have any balls? Mine are flat."

I closed my text. First quarter Modern Mandarin could wait an hour or two.

People say you can tell how a man fucks by watching him on the dance floor. I say it's the tennis court, and Jeremy Coggins played a promising game. He flung himself at every ball. Every shot was hard, intense, and followed through. There was no finesse, but he displayed lots of attractive energy. Sweat was becoming to him.

"Why didn't you go to a college with a forestry program?" I asked after I'd let him win a set and we were resting on a conveniently placed bench.

"Stanford's the family school," he replied glumly. "Anyway, my father would have a heart attack if I were anything but pre-law. What about you? How did you escape Harvard?"

I could have told him my parents didn't really care where I went to college, but I just said, "Lucky me!" and left it at that. He didn't need to know everything about me within the first few days. A little mystery is good for a man.

"Ready for another set?" he asked, jumping up with renewed vigor.

I ran off to my side of the net. "Let's play, tree boy."

***

The next day, there was a message on my phone, inviting me to play tennis at his family's home in San Francisco at the weekend. "Bring your racket and your trunks," he advised. Trunks, I mused. I ran out to Macy's and bought a red speedo. They say dress to impress.

Friday afternoon, we both ditched a class and drove to San Francisco with the top down on 280, the most beautiful freeway I'd ever seen. Trees, lakes, and only a few houses lined the route while we whizzed along at eighty miles an hour. Inside the San Francisco city limits, Jeremy steered us onto a highway along the ocean. The beach ran for miles. I could see what people meant about the ocean here being on the wrong side. It was disconcerting.

We curved northeast into a housing area identified by a discreet entrance sign as the Seacliff neighborhood, headed down an incline to the last house on the street, and passed through an automatic gate. Jeremy left the car in the driveway with the keys inside as the gate closed behind us.

The house was a lengthy, horizontal two stories, with a three-story tower on the windward end, all in bricks of pale brown stone with terracotta roofs. A series of arches across the façade—windows and front door—gave an effect of surprise. The tower was conspicuous against the sky. There was a negligible front yard and no trees that I could see.

A middle-aged servant with Asian features opened the dark wooden front door. I was surprised the family still had a butler in this day and age. We opened our own doors at home. "Hoi," Jeremy said. "This is my friend Andrew Hawthorne." The man looked me over briefly but acutely, bowed slightly, and took our bags with an easy heft of each arm. He had some strength under all that formal attire.

I followed them inside a foyer with uneven, mottled brown flagstones—more a covered courtyard than anything—then through another arch into a long hallway with smooth marble flooring in a color similar to the flagstones. Its walls were lacquered oak, lined with sconces. Every other one was lit. An interesting economy, given the luxury of a butler.

"Mr. Hawthorne will be in the harbor room," the butler told Jeremy. The two exchanged glances. "According to Mrs. Coggins' wishes," he added.

"Well then," Jeremy said, shrugging his shoulders. "Where is she?"

Just then, a beautiful woman appeared, as if on cue. She was as blonde as Jeremy, but had better skin. She swept toward us wearing a rustling skirt, white blouse, and a measured smile.

"Mother! I don't think my friend was expecting anything so grand in the afternoon."

She grimaced at her son. "Charity luncheon. Andy," she said to me and offered her fingers. "Mary Ellen Coggins." A jade bracelet tinkled at her wrist, matched by a jade ring on her right hand. The diamond on her left ring finger was not too large, but certainly not too small. The gold band was plain.

"Mrs. Coggins."

"Mary Ellen," she corrected, her smile thinning. "Jeremy says you're descended from Nathaniel Hawthorne. *The Scarlet Letter* was one of my favorite novels in school. So unfair."

"Yes," I agreed, to all three sentences, my eyes on the cool green jade around her neck.

"I look forward to talking books with you later," she said. "Although," she added, "I hear you're pre-law like my son."

"Lawyers do sometimes read novels," I said, appending a smile.

"Really?" she asked indefinitely and turned to the servant. "Hoi, would you please see our guest to his room?" She gave her son a stare that clearly told him to stay.

Hoi picked up both bags and led me up the stairs. He dropped Jeremy's on the landing, and we continued up a smaller, winding staircase.

My room was a corner suite, although the corner was rounded. It was on the top floor of the tower and simply furnished like the rest of the house, but the fabric patterns were all intricate and the wood looked solid. The room had a 270-degree view with floor to ceiling windows. Filmy drapes were available periodically, but none of them were pulled to. The view swept from the Golden Gate Bridge on my right to a cargo ship in the middle nearing land to the long ocean beach we had driven past. A much smaller beach sat below me at the foot of a rocky cliff. There were trees on this side of the house, down the hill to the beach. Wind had set them to dancing. *Cold,* I thought, and shivered.

"Would you like more heat, sir?" the butler asked. I was surprised he was still with me.

"No," I replied, almost turning into his arms. He took a small step back. "*Xiè xiè,*" I ventured.

"*Bié kèqi,*" he answered with a bemused smile. He explained. "I speak Cantonese, sir, but I understand some Mandarin." My face reddened. He bowed. "I am sorry for embarrassing you. Please forgive me." He raised himself erect. His straight black hair had been combed severely backward against his scalp. Now it sprawled alluringly across his forehead. His high cheekbones, fine nose, and blunt chin all made his face handsome. The lines in his features spoke of character, not age.

"No, please forgive me. I'm studying Mandarin in school. How would you say thank you in Cantonese?"

"It's very close, sir. *Tse tse.*"

"*Tse tse,*" I repeated. Hoi smiled. Smiles were very becoming to him.

We stood, neither of us venturing more. Hoi's demeanor stiffened back into formality. "Shall I put your things away, sir?" he asked, hoisting my bag onto a small bench. He looked at me with openly appraising eyes. I clutched my chest as if I were wearing pearls.

"No, that's all right… Hoi. *Tse tse.*"

I looked out the window again, and this time noticed a pool, tennis courts, and garages partway down the cliff. Close behind me, Hoi startled me by saying, "The pool is heated, sir." After a few moments, he said softly, "Please let me know if there is anything you need," and finally withdrew. He left behind a strong, exotic cologne scent I couldn't place.

I looked out the windows a third time. The northern shore was hilly and ringed by a winding road. I watched cars disappear and reappear. White caps raced each other to the beach below me.

I heard the door open again. It was Jeremy this time, and his predilection for not knocking. He was dressed in tennis shorts and a heavy-looking pullover. He joined me at the windows, standing as close as Hoi had. "It's something, isn't it?" he asked, indicating the bridge with a rightward nod of his handsome head. "I'm so happy we moved here."

"Oh, I assumed this was your family house."

"No, we lived in Orinda until I was twelve. That's in the East Bay. My mother wanted to be in a bigger pond."

"You don't have any siblings?"

"Nope. Just the three of us. And Hoi."

We were alone, and I assumed time was at our disposal. I looked at the king-size bed. Jeremy followed my gaze, flinched, and started walking toward the door. "Be sure to wear something warm," he said. "I'll wait for you downstairs. In the family room. Hoi can show you." After Jeremy's departure, nothing lingered but my urge.

I laughed at myself, got into my tennis garb, and added a jacket. Hoi materialized as I left the room. I followed him silently downstairs, wishing I knew Cantonese or more Mandarin or at least something to say in English. Maybe I could count for him.

Outside, Jeremy and I trekked down the incline to the courts. My legs were cold in the chilly air, but they warmed up quickly in the game. I won in straight sets, 6-2, 6-0. "You were hustling me at Stanford," he said. "Let's go down to the beach."

"What about our rackets?"

"Hoi will take care of them."

We climbed the stairs back to house level. Halfway up, I looked at the windows of my room. Someone was gazing down at us. I pointed this out to Jeremy. "I don't see anybody," he said. "Probably Hoi, putting your things away."

"The person was dressed in white, not black."

Jeremy shrugged. "Maybe he took his jacket off." With that, he walked on. There wasn't anyone at the windows now. Perhaps

I'd been mistaken. Maybe the afternoon light had played a trick on me.

We exited through a metal gate in the thick cream-colored wall separating the Coggins' property from a public right of way. The gate did not shut properly, so I pulled it to. It clicked and locked. Jeremy hurried on past a historical marker. I stopped to read it, but he yelled, "Andy!" up the stairway at me, so I only got as far as the name.

"Why is it called China Beach?" I asked when I caught up with him.

"Chinese fishermen used to land here. Come on. I'll show you." He galumphed further down the stairway, and I galumphed after him.

The beach was small and gloomy, with the great bridge looming surreally large on its right, as if in a painting with improper perspective. We stared at the waves for quite some time without a word of conversation. It was frigid just standing there. When I suggested we return to the house, Jeremy cleared his throat nervously.

"People died out there," he said, nodding at the water. "Chinese fishermen. Their boats sank, or they fell overboard. The bodies washed up on this beach or they brought them to shore here." He seemed oddly serious, much more so than he had been thus far in our short acquaintance.

"That's very sad," I said, which was inane, but I felt I had to respond.

He kicked at the sand. "They say this place is haunted."

"I can believe that," I said. I shivered, but not from fear. I had grown up with spirits whispering Judge Hathorne's sins in my ear at night in my bed, during dark afternoons down empty hallways, or outside in the gloom of New England winters when I played. My sisters never heard them, but ghosts were my old companions.

"I'm serious," Jeremy huffed.

"I'm not afraid of ghosts," I said, leaning toward him conspiratorially. He gave me a long, doleful look. *Enough of this*, I thought. "Let's go up," I suggested and waited for him to proceed so I could enjoy the view of his maximal gluteus maximus.

We climbed silently—except for heavy breathing—until we reached the top. I stopped to finish reading the marker. It verified Jeremy's information, except about the ghosts.

Hoi ushered us silently back inside the house. "Mr. Coggins is home, sir." He observed our tousled hair and bare legs. I'm sure he was scandalized when Jeremy took me into the family room to meet his father. Mr. Coggins was dark to Jeremy's light but, when he shook hands, I felt the family resemblance.

Mrs. Coggins apparently had been reading. There was a book next to her, flattened against the loveseat, spine cracking. "Andy is a Hawthorne, Henry."

Mr. Coggins smiled Jeremy's smile at me. "English major then?"

"No, pre-law."

Mr. Coggins' expression brightened, and Mrs. Coggins went back to reading.

"I graduated from Stanford. Got my law degree there too," Mr. Coggins informed me. "So did my father and grandfather. My great-grandfather graduated from Harvard, though. So did his father." Jeremy rolled his eyes. "You didn't go to Harvard," his father noted.

"Harvard isn't our family school."

"Really? Yale?"

"No, Bowdoin. At least, my part of the family."

Bowdoin College and why I hadn't matriculated there didn't elicit any curiosity from Mr. Coggins. We moved on to a discussion of studying law. Mrs. Coggins closed her book irritably. I noticed the title. *Murder in the Marais.*

"I think I'll go up and dress for dinner," she said. She carried the book with one finger inside to mark the place. More cracking.

"Do you like mysteries then, Mrs. Coggins?" I asked.

"Mary Ellen. Yes, I enjoy a well-plotted one. Do you know Cara Black?" She held the book up for me to see. I said no. She looked disappointed. "Jeremy," she said to her son, discarding me. "We're having dinner in tonight, if that's all right."

Jeremy said, "Fine with us, isn't it, Andy?" and winked at me. I nodded compliantly. Maybe this was a sign we'd be in bed together at evening's end. Why else the wink?

The four of us had drinks back in the family room and dinner in an oversized formal dining room. Its severe white walls were scarcely relieved by scattered family portraits. At least, that's what I assumed they were. Gentlemen in black coats and degrees of facial hair. Ladies in red, pink, and blue dresses down the ages in style. A long walnut table and twelve chairs occupied the center of the room. A double sideboard huddled against the interior wall.

Jeremy had warned me his family dressed for dinner, which struck me as another anachronism about them. I thanked my mother for insisting I pack my tux when I left Massachusetts for college. "Yes, California has a reputation for informality," she agreed. "But what if you want to go to the opera or the symphony? Or the ballet! Better to have it than not," she concluded and patted my hand into compliance. After Jeremy's warning, I sent her a text. She enjoyed being right.

Jeremy and his father were handsome in black and white. His mother was gorgeous in a pink silk sleeveless sheath. "Your dress is beautiful," I told her. "It looks Chinese." Hoi was serving us our dinner. He stopped across from me with a dish of potatoes, his look without an identifiable expression.

"It is," Mrs. Coggins said. She sipped her white wine. "Jeremy told me you're studying Chinese." Hoi was listening, although he now faced away from us at the sideboard.

"Yes, first semester Mandarin."

Mr. Coggins looked amused. "Unusual choice for a lawyer."

Now everyone was listening. Hoi had turned to face me.

"I plan on going into international law. Maybe the diplomatic corps."

"French is still better for that, isn't it?" Mr. Coggins asked.

"My French is good enough for me to get by. I thought Mandarin would be the most practical language these days."

"Interesting," Mr. Coggins said, looking decidedly uninterested. He returned to his steak.

Mrs. Coggins asked me in French how I liked California. Her accent was excellent.

"Very much," I replied, also in French.

"I went to school in France—lycée, then the Sorbonne. How about you?"

"High school French and frequent trips to Canada," I replied. She didn't need to know about my aunt. She laughed, a chiming trill. Her face relaxed. I could see why someone would fall in love with her. "I did have a year abroad as a foreign exchange student."

"Where?"

"Lyon."

"Was it fun?"

"The trips to Paris were." We both laughed and shared happy memories of the City of Light until Mr. Coggins cleared his throat. We switched to English.

When Hoi leaned near me to extend a platter or pour more water or wine, his unusual cologne lingered. I was sure now. It smelled like the seaside when waves and wind rush to the shore. I wasn't much on wearing scent, but I liked this one. I hadn't been much interested in older men either, but there was something increasingly intriguing about Hoi. I began to think Jeremy's equivocal interest might not be important, although I doubted the propriety of having sex with a servant in the Coggins' house. At least, not on the first visit.

After dinner, instead of bed, Jeremy whisked me into town, as he called it, to bars along Chestnut Street in the Marina District. I could still see the bridge. It was west of us now, all lit up, glowing Creamsicle orange in the fog.

"Terrible lot of Republicans here," Jeremy said behind his hand as we walked from his car. "But no one goes to Union Street anymore." There was no mention of the Castro. Maybe I'd misread him. Some men are just flirty. In each new place, he talked with women and avoided eye contact with men.

He brought me back to Sea Cliff before eleven and said good night at the head of the central stairs. There was no invitation to join him in his bedroom on the second floor. I decided any suggestion from me would probably be rebuffed and it was his

Maserati, not mine. I continued up the narrow staircase to the third floor.

Alone again in the odd room, I removed my clothes and hung them, turned the lights out, and went to the windows clad only in my boxers. I scanned the opposite shore. A beacon revolved in a lighthouse there, and lights bobbed in the water in between. Buoys marking the channel. Too bad those Chinese fishermen hadn't had them for guidance. I searched for the beach below me and identified waves striking the shore in curved white lines. I thought of bodies and shivered. Behind me, the door to my room opened with an extended creak. I hadn't misread Jeremy after all! But when I turned, it wasn't Jeremy but a man in a tattered white shirt, ripped pants, and no shoes. These meager clothes clung to his slender body as if they were wet. Long, straight, black hair framed his stricken face. I recognized him.

"Hoi? What happened? Has there been an accident?" The figure staggered toward me. I asked, "Are you hurt?" and rushed across the room, but I pulled up a few feet short. Whoever this person was, he wasn't Hoi. This man was younger, his face frighteningly pallid, eyes molten, pleading. He brushed soggy hair off his unwrinkled forehead. His clothes dripped onto the carpet audibly in the silence of the night.

"Who are you?" There was no response. I tried Mandarin. The young man merely looked around the room, wavering in place. His glance paused at the bed. He took a step toward me, then another. I picked up a book I'd borrowed from the Coggins' bookcases. I hoped a hardcover could do some damage. The stranger reached out to me, mouth open but mute. I raised my arm, ready to bash him with the latest Dan Brown novel, but before I could strike, my visitor's body went limp.

I flung the book away and caught him before he hit the floor. He was cold, so very cold, and thoroughly soaked, with the smell of brine on him. He shivered spasmodically and moaned, a deep, guttural sound. "Let me get you a robe," I said and tried to pull away, but the man clutched at me and kept me close. I tried again, but the keening grew louder, so I let him hold me. I didn't want to wake the family, and, whoever he was, I didn't feel threatened by him any longer.

Our embrace was warming him. His moaning stopped. I could see him better now, so near, in the dim light from outside. He did look like Hoi, only much younger, about my age. My body quickened, and his responded in kind. He said something in a Chinese I couldn't understand, but, when he looked longingly at the bed, I helped him stagger there. Belatedly, I remembered how wet he was and fetched a towel from the en suite, spread it lengthways down the bed and helped him lie down. I wished I could communicate with him.

"Sleepy?" I asked in English and mimed lying my head on prayerful hands. He nodded. When he began shivering, I thought, *linens be damned* and folded my side of the coverlet over him. He smiled a thank you and closed his eyes. I put the robe on against the chill night air seeping through all the windows and sat in one of the chairs in the outer curve of the room. I watched the poor soul fall dead asleep.

In the morning, I awoke in bed, the coverlet over me. I was alone and naked. The bedclothes were dry. The towel was gone.

I remembered part of a dream. I had had sex with my visitor. His body had been warm and dry on top of me, his long fingers and soft mouth busy. I felt him enter me and begin to push...

A knocking at the door interrupted my remembering. The servant's voice asked to come in. "Just a minute," I called out. My frantic eyes found my boxers next to the bed and my robe back in the closet, of course. It had never left it. I had dreamed putting it on. I had dreamed it all.

"Come in," I said when I was covered. The door opened slowly, like last night—in my dream. Hoi stood in his well-fitting uniform with a tray of coffee, toast, and jam. I looked him over carefully. There was a definite resemblance to my nocturnal visitor, except for age. They were Asian, slender but well-built, and about the same height. Both were very good-looking men. "It was a dream," I mumbled.

"What was that, sir?" Hoi asked politely as he poured the coffee. "Room for cream, sir?"

"What? Uh, no. Thank you. I had a dream. That's all. Just a dream," I told him and myself.

He handed me the cup. "A dream, sir? May I ask what it was?"

I thought the question odd and too familiar, but his feet were planted. "All right then," I said with a sigh. "I had a visitor last night. In a dream," I added. "I thought it was you when he appeared."

"Appeared, sir?" Hoi folded his hands behind his back, which thrust his groin forward. His legs were slightly spread apart. I imagined the body beneath the clothes. The scent of the sea rose in the room. Thoughts of the previous night came to mind. I forced those thoughts away.

"Well, not appeared as in poof," I answered with a forced laugh. "He walked through the door. I mean, not through the door. He opened it and walked in." This conversation was making me cranky. I drank some coffee. Maybe that would help.

"What was he wearing, sir?" Hoi asked. Another odd question.

"A ragged white shirt and pants. He was barefoot. And wet."

"Wet?" Hoi asked. Why wouldn't the man take what I said without asking me to repeat everything?

"Drenched," I replied, and drained my cup. I reached for the coffeepot. It was definitely a two-cup morning.

Hoi took the pot out of my hand, poured the refill for me, and inspected the carpet. "There don't seem to be any wet spots, sir."

"I told you it was a dream," I said, my voice rising. I had had enough of this. I sank into a chair and sipped the second cup morosely, wishing he were gone. He seemed to get the hint.

"Will there be anything else, sir?" His dark eyes stared down into mine. They shimmered. I recognized them. His long, straight hair fell over his forehead as he bent closer. I raised my face to meet him. His hand lifted my chin. I remembered his touch. I welcomed his kiss.

"Ready for a swim?" Jeremy asked as he burst into the room. Hoi jerked upright immediately. I gasped loudly. Jeremy ignored us, walked to the windows, and looked in the direction of the bridge. Hoi murmured something Chinese in a low voice and left the room. I had understood what he said. *Later*.

Jeremy turned around. "Be sure to wear your robe and sandals," he said. His look was inscrutable.

***

The pool was heated, as Hoi had promised. Jeremy and I chased each other in feverish laps, then settled into the hot tub for a soak. *Now*, I thought to myself. I was nearly naked in my newly purchased red speedo and Jeremy almost so in his pale green trunks. The garages would shield us from view. It would be easy to slip out of my speedo and help him out of his trunks. No one would know.

Jeremy lounged with arms splayed along the hot tub's edge, head back, eyes closed, a few yards away. I swam-lunged to him. His eyes popped open, displaying fear. "Hello there," he said. His voice trembled. I tried to stroke his wet hair. He pulled away. "Don't," he said, frowning deeply. I lurched away. My heart was pounding now. I expected him to say it was time to get out, dry off, and drive back to Stanford as soon as we both could pack, but he only watched me with what seemed like curiosity, not animosity, and asked, "Did you sleep well last night?" It was a day for odd questions.

"Pretty well."

"Any dreams?"

I made no response.

"Come on. You can tell me." He tried to smile, but it crinkled at the edges and fell. "Come on," he repeated. "Was it about a man in wet clothes?"

That snapped me out of my silence. "As a matter of fact…"

Jeremy interrupted. "I had that dream once. I didn't like it." I watched him sink below the surface of the water.

***

That night, the three Cogginses took me out to dinner, a superb French meal on Nob Hill. Mary Ellen wore another beautiful dress, this one in teal blue shantung silk. We men wore dark, boring suits. Jeremy was animated and cheerful. Our revelatory moment was forgotten—or forgiven. Which didn't matter.

It was late when we set out and later still when we returned. Mrs. Coggins excused herself for bed, but Mr. Coggins, his son, and I shared brandies before we carefully climbed the stairs so as not to disturb Mrs. Coggins, who had the room beneath mine. At the landing, they whispered, "Good night!" at me in unison, and Mr. Coggins turned right to his room, several doors passed Jeremy's. His son kept me with him with a strong hand on my forearm and a cautionary finger against his lips. He waited until his father had disappeared behind his own door, then pulled me toward his room. We stopped just outside.

"You don't have to sleep up there, Andy." His eyes glanced at the upper staircase. This guy was all stop and start. "I could drive you back to the dorm tonight," he finished. Not the invitation I thought was coming after all. Still, I considered his offer. He and I clearly weren't meant to be, and I did have plenty of classwork to do back in Palo Alto.

But it was late, and we had been drinking, so I answered, "In the morning will be fine."

He squeezed my shoulder, which sent a thrill through me in spite of myself. "In the morning then," he agreed.

I climbed the circling staircase slowly. Before the turn, I looked back. Jeremy was still there. He didn't smile. Neither did I. I continued to my room, opened the door, and closed it behind me firmly, leaning against it for good measure. I listened for footsteps coming, but there weren't any. I removed my dress clothes and prepared for sleep, washing my face and brushing my teeth. The image in the mirror looked back at me as blandly as Jeremy had on the landing below. I flicked off the bathroom light and stood at the window again, observing the bridge in the dark one last time. Fog rushed past the window. The great bridge pulsed a muted orange. I went to bed and waited. The door opened and revealed the same pale, pitiful figure from the previous night. I pulled the covers open. He settled beside me, shivering. I knew I could make him warm.

The next morning, I was awake when Hoi knocked on my door. I had already showered and packed.

"You are leaving us, sir?" he asked, setting the coffee tray down on the small table between the armchairs. "The family is having breakfast in the morning room."

"Yes," I replied to the question. I accepted the cup he offered and watched his face while I drank from it. His eyes were warm and loving. *At least something went right this weekend*, I thought.

"I hope you will return soon," he said softly and stayed near me. I considered what to say. Nothing profound came to me, in English or Mandarin. But I had to say something.

"Hoi, do you mind if I ask you a personal question?" The servant nodded deliberately, as if it were a gift. "What does your name mean?"

He lowered his eyes and whispered, "From the sea," and in that moment, just for a moment, I could smell the ocean on him and it was more than cologne. I felt the pull of him, like the outgoing tide. I set down my cup and stood. We embraced, arms grappling like drowning men. Jeremy could burst into the room now. I didn't care. The memory of this would have to last me. I didn't expect any more invitations to spend the weekend in Seacliff.

***

I had breakfast on the first floor with the family. Jeremy told me he'd be ready to leave in a half an hour, which I knew probably meant an hour. Mr. and Mrs. Coggins excused themselves. I was packed and ready. "Why don't you take a walk while you wait?" Jeremy suggested. I considered following Hoi into the kitchen when Jeremy was gone, but the servant unobtrusively shook his head, so I followed Jeremy's suggestion instead.

China Beach was empty at that hour, but warmer than on my first visit. I was not surprised this time by the odd perspective of the bridge. Nor was I surprised by the figure in white at the windows of what had been my room, staring down at me, his hair across his forehead, clothes tattered. I smiled up at him, hoping he saw.

"Ready?" Jeremy asked after I returned to the house. His parents had rejoined us to say goodbye.

"Come back anytime," Mrs. Coggins offered, holding my right hand in both of hers. "*Tu seras toujours le bienvenu.*"

"Yes, anytime," his father echoed. "I can see you're a good influence on my son." I smiled wryly at this. I hadn't wanted to be a good influence, not at all.

Jeremy rolled his eyes, kissed his mother, and gave his father a tap on the shoulder muscle with his fist. Hoi picked up our bags. I knew not to protest. I knew his strength. The three of us walked to the Maserati, which had been perfectly shined. Jeremy slid into the driver's seat and closed his door. Hoi deposited our bags in the trunk. Its lid shielded us from Jeremy's view. His parents had disappeared. "Until next time," he said in a low voice, bowed deeply, and returned to the house.

Back on the beautiful highway along the inaccurately placed ocean beach, Jeremy moved his right hand from the steering wheel to my thigh. "Maybe we could go to Yosemite next weekend," he suggested. "I'm sorry I wasn't very accommodating. It just seemed weird. You know, in my parents' house."

"I'd like that very much."

We drove for some time in silence until a question I needed answering came to mind.

"How long Hoi has been with your family?"

"He came with the house," Jeremy answered, looking perturbed. I moved his hand back to my thigh. He smiled and squeezed. I smiled back and looked west, where celadon waves rushed in, smashing one after the other against the sand, and considered the mystery and reality of men.

Ticket to Ride

It was just an unpainted wooden box, with vertical slats holding up a bale blue sign. Sometimes the sign read "Lemonade 50 cents," only there wouldn't be any lemonade. Other times, it commented on current affairs.

I almost didn't look that morning since I was hurrying to buy something I couldn't live without at Cliff's Hardware, but the message drew my eyes and slowed my steps. "Time machine rides 5 cents, return trip 25 cents." I laughed, put down three dimes, and continued toward Cliff's in a much better mood.

On the way back, my dimes weren't there, but an envelope was, hand-addressed to me. After looks over both shoulders, I shrugged and tore it open. Inside were two rectangles of yellow construction paper. The first said in pencil: *To Wherever*. The second read in ink, *From Wherever. P.S. don't lose*. Each had a disclaimer printed in tiny, precise letters on the back.

"Ticketholder may go to wherever he/she chooses. No time limit on stay. Must have From Ticket to return. (Or else it's not my fault.)"

I thought what a good joke it was until I remembered to wonder how they knew my name. I pondered that awhile, slapping the tickets against my palm. Anyway, if I *were* going to wherever, which wherever would it be?

The answer came to mind immediately. I would go back 30 years, to Chico. I closed my eyes and pictured myself there, but nothing happened, of course. I heard someone say, "Try again." I looked around, but no one was nearby or even grinning from a window. "Out loud," the voice prompted. I stared at the tickets to ride. If I were going crazy, why not go all the way?

"I want to go back to Chico when I was 18 before…"

In the middle of my sentence, my head jerked. I saw my room in Chico and me lying on my rumpled bed, breathing heavily. And then I was there.

"Aaron," I heard my father call, which almost made me cry since he'd been dead nearly twenty years. Next, he'd bang on the door and yell "breakfast!"

Bang, bang, bang! "Breakfast!" I jumped out of bed, pulled on my boxers, and opened the door.

"Dad!" I yelled, grabbing him in a bear hug.

"Hey, big guy!" he said in surprise. "What's the occasion?" I held on until he pulled away, hands on my shoulders. "What's wrong, son?"

"Nothing, Dad," I told him and pulled him close again, smelling his aftershave, feeling the scratch of his stubble on my cheek. He patted my shoulder. Neither of us knew what to say. Neither of us ever did. Finally, Dad pulled away again, and I let him go.

"You better get dressed, son. Your mother's champing at the bit. Remember, we're going to the coast today after breakfast. You sure you want to stay here on your own? It's gonna be a scorcher."

"Yeah," I said uncertainly. Why exactly was I staying home?

"You and Kevin don't tear up the place, okay? No wild parties." Oh, right. It was *that* weekend.

I went across the hall to the bathroom I used to share with my little brother, and there he was, brushing his teeth. He looked back at me in the mirror. "Don't say it," he mumbled through the toothpaste.

"What?"

"You always ask, 'Why ya brushing your teeth *before* breakfast?' and then you mess up my hair."

"Okay, I won't ask. Anyway, Ben, it's your mouth." He was still staring at our faces in the mirror. "What?" I asked again.

"You called me Ben."

"That's your name, isn't it?"

"A million times I ask you to stop calling me Benny and you never do. Why today?"

He was right. I didn't call him Ben until he went in the Army. "Yeah? Must be your lucky day… Benny." He made a face, showing me all the toothpaste in his mouth, and went back to brushing.

I hopped in the shower. When I opened the door and reached for my towel, it was gone, and so was Ben. Funny guy. I dried off as best I could with the hand towel.

The mirror was all mine. Damn, I used to have a lot of hair! Now I was about as bald as Dad and Grampa. *Grampa.* He was gone too. I combed my long, luxurious hair and ran to get dressed.

When I walked into the kitchen, my family was eating pancakes, like we did almost every Saturday back then. I sat down to mine, wondering what chores my dad would have for me while they were away. On cue, he said, "Be sure to mow the lawn today, son."

"I will, Dad," I promised, glad to use the word *Dad* again.

"Then, and only then, can you and Kevin go for a swim in the pool." That's right. Dad had the pool put in that spring, in time for summer.

I got the mower out of the garage and yanked the cord to get it going. The noise was louder than I remembered. I had almost finished the section between the two crepe myrtles when my family came trooping out the front door. I cut the motor and brushed the hair out of my eyes. I still did that sometimes, even though it was just phantom hair.

"Here's the number of the motel we're staying at," my mother said. I stared at her hand. It was so smooth and pale. Now it was wrinkled and mottled with liver spots.

Dad handed me some money. "Enjoy yourself." I pocketed the bills, realizing my wallet was 30 years ahead of us in San Francisco.

"We'll be back late Sunday," Mom said as she got in the front passenger seat of the old Buick. Benny slid in back. I waved goodbye and stared after them. Dad was dead, Mom was in a retirement 'village,' and Benny lived in Massachusetts. Maybe I should have gone with them. But that wasn't why I came back. I cranked the mower up again.

Once I'd finished the backyard, I reached in my pocket to let Kevin know my family was gone. Oh, right. No cell phones yet.

"Hello?" Kevin's voice answered after I called him from our house phone. My brain couldn't get my mouth to work. "Aaron, is this you?" he asked after I just kept breathing into the handset.

I wanted to shout "I love you! I'm sorry!" over and over, but all I said was, "Yeah. How ya doing?"

"Great. Your folks gone?" Kevin was always a get down to business kind of guy.

"Yeah."

"Okay. See you in ten. Bye!"

The dial tone buzzed in my ear. I was about to see my dead lover. What would I say to him after what I'd done? Only, I hadn't done it yet.

It seemed like only seconds before the Mustang's tires screeched when Kevin hit the brakes in our driveway. The car door slammed, his big feet slapped along the sidewalk, the doorbell rang, and there he was, all six-foot-three, 220 pounds of him, in sleeveless shirt, baggy shorts and flipflops. I resisted the urge to throw my arms around him and cover him in kisses. Neighbors in a small town are always watching, and Kevin wasn't out back then. Neither was I.

"Why'd you ring the doorbell?" I asked, hands inserting themselves into my jeans shorts.

"I always ring the doorbell." Something else I'd forgotten. That said, he closed the door behind him and leaned down to kiss me with those soft, full lips no one would forget. "You wanna?" he asked, wiggling his eyebrows.

"Uh, let's go for a swim first."

"Huh?" He looked at me like I was crazy. Maybe I was. I mean, was any of this really happening? But he felt real when he put his arms around me, so I wiggled my eyebrows yes.

"That's better, baby," he said and led me off to the bedroom. We got undressed and into bed. Kevin took his time. Nobody was home to knock or walk in on us. But, when he lifted my legs in the air, I said, "Not without a condom."

He looked at me like I was crazy. "Condom? Are you worried I'll make you pregnant?" He laughed; I didn't. "Aw, come on, Aaron!" I sat up, crossed my legs, and folded my arms across my chest. "Shit," he mumbled, getting out of bed. I was afraid he was leaving. He was.

"Shit," he repeated, getting back into his clothes. "I'll be back as fast as I can."

***

He threw the open box of Trojans on the nightstand and nearly ripped off his clothes. He already had a rubber in hand. After sex, we lay naked on top of the bed, him smoking those damn cigarettes, one arm around my shoulders, my head against his.

"I wish you weren't going away this summer."

I was going away? Oh, right. The Forest Service. Oh, no! Geoff! "I have to make money for college," I said, like there hadn't been a pause. "And you've got football camp, anyway." We were going to UCLA. I wanted to go to Berkeley, but he had talked me out of it. UCLA was a better football school.

"Yeah, I know, but that's not till August. You coulda taken the road trip with me."

The past came back to me with a thud. After this weekend, I had spent that summer cutting brush with a machete and chain saw and fucking Geoff Freudlich. Kevin had ridden the Harley around eleven Western states before he went off to UCLA. I had gone to Berkeley, after all, with Geoff.

"Come visit me in Arcata," I suggested.

"I am. Hey, what's with you today?" He stubbed the cigarette out on an empty coke can and turned towards me, his fingers automatically attaching themselves to my left nipple. "You're gonna miss this, baby. And this." He put his other hand on my cock and started jerking.

"I sure have," I said, gasping.

He laughed. "You talk like it's been years or something."

"Yeah," I agreed, making myself laugh too.

It always amazed me the All-North State quarterback fucked me on a regular basis. After our second go, he looked down at me, leering. "You sure are horny today, babe. Whew," he said, flopping against the mattress. When he reached for another cigarette, I tried to stop him. He slapped my hand away, lit up, took a puff, and asked, "So, what do you wanna talk about?"

I gulped. My ticket to ride had brought me back to Wherever all right, the last minutes before I'd ruined my life, before I told Kevin I didn't want to go to UCLA, that I thought we should break up. What should I say instead? Kevin smoked while I thought.

"Knock, knock," he said, rapping his knuckles against my forehead.

"Uh… well… I just thought maybe we should make some plans for your visit. To Arcata, I mean." Good save, Aaron. Everything would be all right now. It had been so simple. I could go back to 2020 soon.

"Oh, yeah. We should decide when and where. I gotta fit it into the ride."

We settled on a date. As for where, I said, "I have a room," remembering Mrs. Grundy's big, white, two-story house. "I'll give you the address."

"Yeah, I'll need it to drive you up there like we planned." He took a drag on the cigarette and blew the smoke away from us. It hovered in the air at the foot of the bed like the specter it was. In 18 years, he'd be lying in a different kind of bed. I yanked the cigarette out of his mouth and pushed it down the Coke can.

"Hey! Why'd you do that?"

"You know why. Cigarettes are going to kill you."

Kevin slumped and stared up at the ceiling. "Yeah, I know. I *know*," he said, looking at me. "I've tried to quit. I can't."

"You can. You will. Otherwise, you're dead at 36."

"What, you have a vision or something? Sounds like you know the exact date."

I did. Where was a nicotine patch when you needed one? Not invented yet. I could probably "invent" all kinds of stuff. We could be millionaires.

"Earth to Aaron. Come in, please." Kevin was waving his hand in front of my face. I blinked. We were still on my bed, totally naked, his big football body still muscular and full of life. And his beautiful hair. I ran my fingers through it. He closed his eyes and hummed happily.

"Baby, when did you start doing that?" His eyes opened. "Okay, let's make our plan." It was back to business.

***

Kevin drove me the 200 miles to Arcata in the Mustang, with me playing GPS. Mom and Dad offered to take us, but I needed to be alone with Kevin as much as possible before I met Geoff for the second time.

The house was at the end of a cul-de-sac. Huge blackberry bushes filled the lot behind the gravel parking area next to the kitchen porch. I was looking forward to seeing Mrs. Grundy again, remembering how nice she was to me that summer. I'd been so unhappy when I arrived. The Mustang sent the gravel flying as Kevin stomped on the brakes just before he ran over the blackberries. He hopped out, popped the trunk, and hoisted both my bags out.

"Let me take one."

"Nah. I got 'em." He looked towards the porch and turned on his Mr. Popularity smile. A friendly looking older woman smiled back at him.

"Aaron?" she asked, looking at Kevin.

"I'm Aaron, Mrs. Grundy," I said, moving toward her. "This is my friend Kevin."

"Welcome to Arcata, both of you! Let me show you to your room, Aaron. It's upstairs," Mrs. Grundy said in her always optimistic-sounding voice. We followed her into the house and up the narrow flight of steps, down the equally narrow hall. At the farthest room, she turned the knob. "I'm sorry, there's just the one bed."

"That's okay," Kevin said, trying not to grin. I was glad Geoff wouldn't arrive until the next week.

Mrs. Grundy opened the door and showed us the one bed, which was occupied at the moment by a large, well-built, dark-haired person about my age. Geoff was here already! I must not have remembered correctly.

Mrs. Grundy looked flustered, too. "Oh, Geoff! I'm sorry. I was just showing...oh well, Geoffrey Freudlich, this is your roommate, Aaron Cohen. You're both working for the Forest Service this summer."

Geoff stood up in his t-shirt and tighty whities, displaying a body I definitely had not forgotten. He rapidly covered it with a robe, shook my hand, then reached out to Kevin, whose mouth was wide open.

"Uh, this is my friend Kevin Roberts." I tried to look at Geoff like we were strangers.

Kevin closed his mouth, put my bags down, and shook Geoff's hand, squeezing hard enough for Geoff to wince. In return, Geoff squeezed harder, and Kevin grimaced. They had locked hands like two bulls competing for the same cow. Finally, Kevin said, "I gotta go," and lurched away. I followed, trying to talk to him as he tromped down the hall and pounded down the stairs. He finally answered me outside by the Mustang.

"Where am I going to stay, Aaron? In bed with you and your roomie? I don't think so."

"We could get a motel room. Please, Kevin. Don't be mad. Geoff wasn't supposed to be here until next week."

"Oh, it's Geoff already, huh?"

Damn. Blew it already. "Don't be jealous," I said, trying to recover.

"I'm not jealous," he said automatically. He leaned against the car. "Okay, I'm jealous." A big sigh lifted his big chest. He looked up at the second floor. "It's a long summer."

"Don't worry," I said, giving him a hug and kiss out in public. "I love you, remember?"

"Wow," Kevin said. "Who are you, and what did you do with my boyfriend?" I pulled away fast, and he grinned. "Yeah, I remember. I love you too, babe," he said, socking my shoulder.

"I'll come through on the bike like I promised. Then, we'll be together at college and next year we can get our own place. What's one summer, anyway?" Kevin had life planned out for us, down to his career and mine. He would play in the N.F.L., and I would be a doctor. I knew the N.F.L. wouldn't be ready for an openly gay quarterback in 1988, but we wouldn't have to face that situation, anyway. Kevin would become a copier salesman after college and work his way up at Xerox. He was their youngest district manager when he died.

"Right," I agreed, trying not to picture his funeral.

"Don't look so sad, baby. I saw a phone in the kitchen. We'll talk." He gave me another hug and a kiss with plenty of tongue before he hopped in the car and drove away, honking three times like always. When there was only empty street and settling dust, I wiped my eyes and turned around to face the house. No one was staring or calling the police. I went inside.

Mrs. Grundy was in the kitchen, too obviously stirring a pot. She looked around at me. "Is everything all right, dear?"

"Yes," I assured her—and myself. "It's just that my friend had planned to stay the weekend." The lie the words *my friend* told hovered in the air between us.

"Oh, I'm sorry. I wish I had another room but, when the Forest Service called, I told them I only had the double bed. I thought they'd tell you." I said it was okay even though it wasn't and began trudging up the stairs to start avoiding my summer fate.

The door was open, and Geoff was sitting on the bed wearing shorts and a tight tee shirt when I walked in. He stood up.

"I hope everything is okay, Aaron."

"Don't worry about it."

"I'm sorry about the bed. I didn't know either until I got here. I called the Forest Service, but they said basically take it or leave it." I thanked him for trying.

He indicated the chest of drawers. "I saved half for you. You want the top or bottom?"

"Huh?"

"Do you want the top two drawers or the bottom two?"

"Bottom, I guess."

He gave me that lopsided grin I had loved so much the two years we'd dated at Berkeley. "Good. I'd rather be on top, anyway."

"Uh, okay," I said, looking away. My eyes landed on my luggage.

"Here. Let me help you with those." He yanked both bags onto the bed as if they were Ziplocs. I bent over and started unpacking, trying not to sweat. He stood behind me, and the room temperature went up even higher. I kept unpacking.

"Well, I guess I better get out of your way," he said after several minutes of mutual silence. I said okay without turning around. Once I heard the stairs creak, I sat on the bed and asked myself how I was going to do this.

That night, Geoff made it even more difficult when he invited me to dinner. Mrs. Grundy cooked breakfast for her boarders, but at lunch and dinner we were on our own. I tried to say no, but Geoff wore me down, just like he always did.

At Angelo's, we sat across from each other like we were on a first date, which in 1984 we had been, as it turned out. Geoff was a good listener and matter of fact about himself. He was a sophomore at Berkeley and on the baseball team—no scholarship. His dad owned a chain of department stores. I recognized the last name. He asked lots of questions about Kevin, except the one I knew he really wanted the answer to.

Back at the house, Mrs. Grundy was watching "Family Ties" on her new Sony in the living room. I thought about Michael J. Fox's future with Parkinson's and felt sad for him. Geoff and I said good night to her and went upstairs.

"You want the bathroom first?" he asked. "Hey, you like hiking? There are some great trails around here." I gulped and said no. We had had a wide variety of sex on some of those great trails. I collected my toiletries and went first at brushing my teeth. Back in our room, Geoff was sitting on the bed with just a towel wrapped around him. His chest was everything I remembered.

"All done?" he asked, hopping up.

"Yep," I said, in what I hoped sounded jaunty instead of nervous.

I waited for him to leave, only he didn't. He just stood there in his towel, watching me standing there in mine. His started to tent. So did mine.

"I can't," I said quietly.

"Boyfriend?" he asked, and I nodded. "The guy today?" I nodded again. "Too bad." He rewrapped his towel, so his erection was against his body, took one more look at mine, and left for the bathroom. I exhaled, slipped back into my Jockeys, and got into bed. When Geoff came back, he turned off the light. I heard the towel drop and his underwear slide on. I remembered how good his ass felt inside it.

"Ouch!"

He must have bumped into something.

"You can turn the light back on."

"It's okay."

I listened to him settle into bed and not say anything for several minutes. I was drifting off to sleep when I heard him whisper, "I wish you didn't have a boyfriend."

I wanted to say, "Me too," but just pretended I didn't hear.

The next morning, we were spooning when I woke, my ass against his erection, his arm holding me close. That summer, Geoff and I fell asleep like that almost every night and woke up in the same position almost every morning. We fit together well, but then so did Kevin and I. *Kevin.* I tried to pull away, but Geoff mumbled something in his sleep, and his arm tightened around me. I tried again and woke him up.

"Oh, God! I'm sorry. I was asleep. Really!"

"I know."

The second night it happened, I said, "I could get a sleeping bag."

He leaned over me. "Maybe we could put pillows down the middle of the bed or something."

"That won't leave much room, especially for you." I sat up while he considered that. "Look," I said. "We can do it. We don't have to have sex."

He gave me his crinkly smile. "Then, won't it be more like not doing it?" So, we spent the weeks before Kevin came back not doing it, although anyone who saw us and knew from gays, assumed we were. We worked together, ate all our meals together, shopped together, and slept together, his erection against my ass every morning. Mrs. Grundy treated us like a couple. People in Arcata stared at us. The surveyors we worked for made insinuations. Frequently.

By the time Kevin called to remind me when he'd be back in Arcata, I was so horny I was ready to jump him in the blackberry bushes. I booked a motel room instead.

"Hey, this is a nice room," he said as he opened the door. I closed it behind us and started kissing him fast and furiously, then went down on him. "Wow! I missed you too, babe!" he yelped.

Post second coitus, I lay on his chest, waiting for him to light up, but he didn't.

"Three weeks, no smokes," he said, grinning at me. "Do I get a reward?"

***

Another month passed, with Kevin in Chico working for his dad and me in Arcata working for my Uncle Sam. We talked every day, which really ran up Mrs. Grundy's phone bill since I usually dialed the numbers. But reminding myself I loved Kevin was the only way I couldn't fall in love with Geoff again.

When we all turned the calendar to August, Kevin flew south for football camp at UCLA, no cars allowed. Phone calls got fewer. Geoff and I got closer. When he told me about his life at Berkeley, I remembered more than he said. It had been our life after all, once upon a time.

Not having sex became increasingly difficult for both of us. One Saturday morning, it proved impossible. I got a sleeping bag after that. Geoff said he'd sleep on the floor, but I made sure we took turns.

At the end of August, my last day in the Forest Service and taking turns on the floor finally arrived. Football camp was over, and Kevin was flying north to pick up his car, pick up his boyfriend, and drive both of us back to Westwood. I was going to be a tennis team walk-on, so he and I could be roommates in the jocks' dorm.

Geoff and I said goodbye at a gas station off 101 in Arcata. After they gassed up, he and the surveyors were driving to Gasquet for the rest of the week.

"Thanks for everything!" he said, with what looked like tears in his eyes. The surveyors glanced at each other like, yep, homos. I didn't care anymore. I leaned across the seat and gave Geoff a long hug. I wanted to say let's keep in touch but just got out and waved goodbye.

The green Forest Service SUV pulled out of the gas station, and I ran up the overpass sidewalk. From the center of it, I watched the SUV merge onto 101 north. I waved again in case Geoff was looking back. Then, I walked the long, sad blocks to Mrs. Grundy's.

Kevin was waiting outside the house. I tried to smile for him. He looked so happy and healthy. He hadn't smoked all summer. Seeing him, I knew I'd made the right decision coming back, not changing our plans, not screwing up my life and his.

"I put your bags in the trunk already," he told me. "You good to go?"

"I'll just say goodbye to Mrs. Grundy."

"She had to leave. She told me to give you a big hug." I hugged him back so tightly I could feel his heart beating. He gave me a deep kiss, and I didn't worry about the neighbors.

"I'll just go in and take another look around," I said after he let me go.

"Okay, babe. Take your time." Old Kevin would have pulled his pack out then and had a smoke while he waited, but New Kevin just settled his bubble butt against the Mustang, folded his arms across his chest and smiled.

The house was locked, so I used my key. After writing my note to Mrs. Grundy, I wandered around, saying a bittersweet goodbye to both summers, the one before my ticket to ride and the one after.

In my room with Geoff, I looked at the bed we'd slept in and, once, made love in. I felt a tsunami of regret and, for better or worse, also wrote him a note, providing my address and phone number. In the final moments, I couldn't face not knowing him. And anyway, I'd be safe and sound in Los Angeles with Kevin. It wasn't like I'd be living in that funny old house on Channing Way.

On my way out, I stopped at the kitchen window. Through the curtains, I could see Kevin still leaning against the Mustang, trying not to be impatient. I could also see Geoff's MG farther away, out where he always parked it, so it wouldn't get dented. What would all our lives be like, now that I had changed the past? Would I still know Geoff? Would Kevin start smoking again? And my dad. If he just ate healthier food, got more exercise, and had his cholesterol checked, he wouldn't have his stroke, at least not so soon.

I pulled the return ticket out of my wallet and read the words again. I had come back to change my life, and I had. The thing was, I would never actually get to live that life. But I could. I only had *not* to do just one more thing. I heard Kevin honk the horn, a bugle call to action.

Without another thought, I tore my return ticket in half, quarters, and eighths and let the pieces flutter into the trashcan under the sink. My stomach dropped with them. What had I done? Kevin honked again. I looked outside. He was walking toward the door.

"I'm sorry," I said, opening it for him.

"No problem," he lied, one foot tapping.

I locked the kitchen door behind us, slipped my key through the mail slot, and took my first steps into the next 30 years. I wasn't sure what would happen through all those years, but I was ready to find out. Kevin opened the passenger door on the Mustang, and I slid in. He popped the gearshift into reverse, backed up, and off we roared, leaving dust and gravel flying behind us. I settled into my seat. I no longer had a ticket, but I was ready to ride.

The Cowman and the Farmer Should Be Friends

It's lonely being a dairy farmer in West Marin, especially if you're a gay one. I grew up on my parents' place near Point Reyes Station. My Tomasi great-grandfather started the farm and handed it down. My plan is to be the fourth-generation dairy farmer in our family. What can I say? I like milk.

Being gay crept up on me. I dated girls in high school but suspected I played for the other team. Too much interest in other boys' bodies in gym class and after-school sports. In college, my suspicions were confirmed.

My boyfriend at Cal Poly was a would-be civil engineer. After I graduated with a four-year B.S., he decided he would rather finish his engineering degree than follow me back to West Marin. I didn't blame him; he had his fifth year to get through. We stayed in touch but, after he accepted a job in San Diego, I knew we were done. In hindsight, maybe a future veterinarian would have been a better dating choice.

I came out to my parents in college but felt shy about bringing someone home while I was living in their house. Who knew if I was bringing home a murderer? When I needed sex or companionship of my own kind, I hopped on my Honda and took an invigorating ride down Highway 101 to San Francisco. So what if I had helmet hair when I arrived? I'm tall and blond, with plenty of milk-fed muscles.

One day, however, Dad said, "How'd you like to have your own place?" I thought he was telling me it was time to leave, the papa bird shoving the baby bird out of the nest.

"Can I still work on the farm? Or are you selling the place?"

Dad put his hands on his waist, leaned back, and guffawed so loudly Mom came out on the porch to see if he was okay. "No, son. Your own house. I was thinking down by the intersection would be good. We could even build you a garage, in case you ever give up the motorcycle and buy a vehicle with a roof."

"It would give you more privacy," Mom added, in case I didn't catch the drift of the conversation.

The house my dad had built for me is no mansion, just four rooms with a mud porch and a bathroom, but it's fine for me. Sadly, though, it didn't help my sex life much. It's not easy convincing people to ride seventy minutes on the back of a Honda CB750, so we can fuck in my bed instead of theirs. Some people are adventurous though, especially the ones into Western drag.

"Are you, like, a cowboy?"

"Dairy farmer," I reply. That frequently dampens their enthusiasm, which usually takes another hit once we reach dairy country.

"What's that smell?"

"Cows," I answer. The next morning, after I do my chores and give them breakfast, my visitors usually ask to leave. On the outbound trip, they hug me so tightly I can barely breathe. On the inbound, it's a different story—and not one with a happy ending.

I did have a sort of relationship for a couple of years with one of our hired men. Ramon was also in his twenties. Short, cute, and a bottom in bed. I was a happy man. The Honda didn't get much highway use after Ramon joined me under the covers. The problem was he had a wife and two kids back in Sonora and the day came when Mrs. Ramon got tired of excuses why she and the kids couldn't join *el marido* north of the border. A cousin or a brother showed up, put one and one together, came up with the two of us, and sent his findings to the wife. Soon after, Ramon got an email he didn't share with me. He headed south the next day.

So, at 28, I was back on the Honda on my way to San Francisco. I kept this up for another two years because sex was worth it but, when I hit thirty, I began to think it wasn't. My folks noticed I was spending Saturday nights in West Marin and didn't seem to be dating anyone local. They were in their sixties and worrying about me being alone after they left—not that they were expecting to die anytime soon. No, they were planning to travel when they reached sixty-five—not something you can do much of when you have cows to care for.

"Did you know Helen Zamastil has a gay nephew?" my mother asked one night over dinner. I continued to chew my peas. "Yes," she said, in spite of my disinterest. "She told me Saturday at the Farmers Market in San Rafael." I took a last bite of salad and tried to ignore my mother's stare. "Helen says

Jeff's very nice. She sent me a photo." Her phone intruded into my line of sight. I took a quick look to make her happy. A surprisingly good-looking young man smiled back at me. My look got longer. "He's a CPA." I got up to rinse my plate and stow it in the dishwasher.

"I'm not asking Helen Zamastil's nephew out."

"Why not? He has his own car."

"What's that got to do with it?"

"You wouldn't have to buy one," my father noted. "Not everyone wants to ride on the back of a motorcycle."

"Don't I know," I agreed. "Look, I'm sure Jeff Zamastil is nice, and his car is nice, but I'm not asking anyone out right now. I'm happy the way I am." My mother tried to bolster her argument in favor of Helen's nephew, but I held up a hand. "No," I said, to keep it simple. She looked at my father for reinforcements. He shrugged. She looked back at me, sighed, and put away her phone.

A few days later, she opened a second front. "Did you ever try online dating? I hear OKCupid works really well."

"How do you know about OKCupid?"

"Oh, Marjorie Andersen told me all about it. Her daughter Aileen used it, and now she's getting married."

"I don't want to get married."

"Why not? You can. Anyway, Marjorie told me that OKCupid is for gay people, too."

My mother and Marjorie Andersen clearly had discussed this at length, which was more worrisome than my mother and Helen Zamastil conjuring up an unattached nephew for me at the farmers' market. But, although I didn't want marriage, I *was* feeling the need for masculine companionship, so I said I'd think about it. "No promises though."

When Dad also brought up dating apps that evening—probably at my mother's instigation—I gave up. "Okay," I said. "I'll try a dating site." My parents nearly cheered.

I did some research before bed and found one that's 100% gay and rural. I told them the next morning over breakfast. "GayFarmersAreUs."

"Gay Farmers what?" my father asked. "You made that up." I whipped out my phone and brought up the website. My parents leaned close.

"Well, I'll be," my father said. "They've got everything online these days."

But my mother tried one more time. "Audrey Macomb says—"

"Mom, I don't care what Audrey Macomb, Marjorie Andersen or, for that matter, Helen Zamastil says. I'm using GayFarmersAreUs. I figure it might increase my odds of finding a guy who can deal with life on a dairy farm."

My mother shook her head at her lap. She clearly had her heart set on OKCupid.com, but I had made my decision. I completed the interminable online questionnaire and narrowed my area of interest to north of the Golden Gate. I hoped this would mean I'd meet men who wouldn't mind driving fifty miles and would know what to expect when they got here. Right away, I got a lot of responses, mainly from much younger men. Apparently, without me knowing it, I had graduated to the daddy stage of gay male life. I was in my thirties, gainfully employed, and still in shape. But enough men in my own age bracket did check me out and engage in online flirtation for me to start going out on dates.

My first guy was a wine wrangler from Sonoma. He was in his late thirties and, from his photo, sort of cute. Unfortunately, it wasn't a recent snapshot. When he showed up, the liver spots were a dead giveaway. We had a cup of coffee and a nice chat. He asked me out again. Since I wanted to be an equal opportunity employer, I said yes. The next weekend, I spent an hour at a nice restaurant in Petaluma all by myself when Ed didn't show up. Some men just have to win, no matter what the game is.

Bachelor #2 was also interested in wine. He drank a lot of it. I had learned from Bachelor #1, so, when #2 suggested we have a second date, I said *no* quickly, but very politely.

Bachelors Three through Twelve went by in a blur. They were all legitimately in their thirties or forties, reasonably nice looking, and fairly pleasant, but with no distinguishing characteristics. I do remember a few moments. There was the guy who sat next to me on the couch and kept looking at my hair. He got pissed when I said, "It's real" and left without saying goodbye. Another fellow brought a dozen donuts as a hospitality gift and ate most of them. I had sex with one just because he was hot, but no emotional sparks flew.

I didn't seem to have any trouble finding dates, but it was definitely quantity, not quality. One unifying principle was that dairy farming was fine on paper, but not in fact. If their nose wrinkled or they outright coughed on arrival when they came to visit, I knew it would not be lasting love. Another commonality was no one was involved in animal husbandry except me. They farmed rice or almonds or wine. I began to consider trying a different website, maybe even OKCupid.

Bachelor 13 at least raised four-legged animals—sheep—in Sonoma County near the ocean. On our first date, we had a nice enough dinner at a bistro cafe of his choice in Sebastopol, after which I followed him to his place on the coast. He had barely closed the door before he was stripping and leading me down the hallway into bedroom territory. His clothes dotted the way in case I got lost. I discarded my own clothing when we were closer to the bed.

"Not bad," #13 said when my chest came into view. When I took my jeans off, he mused, "Nice thighs," but, when my Jockeys slipped down my legs, it was just, "Hmm." That was a little demoralizing, but 13 hopped onto the bed, so I assumed he was still interested.

The play-by-play during our 'love' making continued to be judgmental and distracting. I suggested he keep his comments nonverbal. He did, and we completed our mission. He asked me to stay overnight and come back the next weekend. I did, thinking things could only get better now he knew I didn't appreciate the color commentary.

How wrong we can be. 13 and I cooked the evening meal together, and I used too much salt. At dinner, I could tell my table manners did not meet the genteel expectations of a sheepherder. On the third date, he didn't like the shirt I was wearing and insisted I change to one of his for our dinner and a movie. And of course, his monologue during sex started up again during date two and continued through date three without a commercial break, even after I told him again it was a downer and asked him to stop. At least I was earning higher marks and the sex, even with 13's commentary, was pretty good.

On the fourth date, he asked me to stay the weekend, and I made the mistake of saying yes. We lurched from one disaster to the next—culinary, clothing, and commentary. Even the sex was bad. Sunday morning, I used the cows as an excuse to go home before another home-cooked meal, which I wouldn't be, I was informed, allowed to help with.

Once I got inside my own four walls, I sent 13 an it's-me-not-you email, even though it *was* him. A few words of advice. If you meet a guy named Steve who raises sheep in Sonoma County, walk away fast without looking back.

After that, I decided to take a break from homosexual dating, which meant from dating altogether since I wasn't AC DC. It was just as well. Victor, one of our two hired men, had taken a job as a fry cook in San Rafael, which left just Pablo, Dad, and me, so I wouldn't be able to do any more sleepovers for a while. I put a job ad online for a new hand and ignored messages from GayFarmersAreUs that averred, "He's checking you out right now!" or "Five matches just for you!"

Of course, I did keep looking at photos on the site. I figured window-shopping wouldn't hurt and, after hours of attaching and detaching milking machines to 600 teats, a man does have needs. Two photos stood out. The same guy was in both. In one, he was frontal, wearing a cowboy hat, a big smile, tight faded jeans, and an equally tight red t-shirt. The second was a back view, so you had a full 360. He was strapping in both directions. I referred to his photos several times over the coming days to help with my needs.

I tried to keep my stimulation visual but finally read his profile. His name was Ben, and he lived in eastern Oregon, about "twenty miles from the nearest town." Man, he was worse off than I was. And eastern Oregon? How had this guy snuck past my fifty-mile perimeter? And he was only twenty-two. But the memory of Ben's chest and butt motivated me to read on.

Oregon State University, degree in animal husbandry. A gong went off in my brain. Worked with his dad and brothers on the family cattle ranch. Interested in living closer to civilization. Being gay in eastern Oregon was probably even lonelier than in West Marin. Besides, he was awfully cute and willing to relocate, so I sent him a message. He sent a funny one back, which made me laugh several times, and there we were, having an extended online conversation.

Ben suggested we talk by Skype, so I downloaded the ap and wondered what to wear besides a work hat. Maybe that would be enough. I had taken to lifting weights to burn some of the sexual energy, and the results had been outstanding, if I do say so myself. But starting out naked wasn't in my DNA. I decided on a tight t-shirt and jeans, both blue to match my eyes.

I was nervous about getting the time wrong. The Foster ranch was so far east in Oregon, it was in a different time zone.

"Wow!" Ben said when he came on the screen. "You look just like your photos."

"And you're surprised by that?"

"I wondered about the blond hair."

"Why? It's real."

"Well, you being Italian."

"Northern Italian." That didn't seem to register, but I wasn't interested in filling him in on the demographics of Italy, south to north. "Anything else?"

He blushed. How old was he again? "Not really." He huffed himself up. "You know, people lie."

"You didn't."

"I wasn't brought up that way."

"Me either. Which church?"

"Baptist. How about you?"

"I'm a Catholic."

There was a distinct pause before he said, "Well, at least you're a Christian." *Christian*, I thought. *What's with this guy?* He looked off in the distance like a squirrel or something had caught his eye. "So…," he drawled. "I'm glad you liked my pictures."

"You have a great body."

He blushed again. "I work out some. Not a lot else to do around here. You look like you have a good body, too." I started to take off my shirt to show him the details. "No, no!" he yelled. "My folks might come in!"

My first thought was, *the door doesn't have a lock on it?* "Sorry," I assured him, tugging my shirt back down. At least he got to see my abs.

There was another long pause, this time from my side. Should I say goodbye or continue the conversation? I decided to continue. He was cute and hot, and I was horny. I brought up animal husbandry, and he became more verbal. We managed to discuss dairy cattle versus beef cattle for fifteen minutes before he said he had to go. He severed the Skype connection before I could say goodbye.

I wondered what would happen next. I knew what I hoped would happen, although it seemed a little creepy. Doesn't everything you say and do on screen sit out there in the ether somewhere, waiting to be revealed to all seven billion humans on the planet? We hadn't made a second Skype date, anyway. I decided to let the universe decide.

A couple of days later, I received a message from Skype. Ben F. wanted to talk. I let my bedroom blinds down and typed that I was available. He appeared on the screen. Shirtless. I nearly fell off the bed.

"I've been thinking about last time," he said, with a coy expression on his face. I didn't think his mind had been on animal husbandry. "You know, when you wanted to take your shirt off for me." I nodded to keep him going. "Well, maybe you'd do that—" My t-shirt was gone before he could finish the sentence. His eyes bulged. "You're hairy."

I resisted the urge to put my shirt back on and asked, "Is that bad?"

"No?" he said, like it was a question. We stared at each other's chests across the miles. Who would make the next move? Anybody?

The matter was settled by a deep voice off camera. "Benjamin?"

Ben yelled back. "I'm on Skype."

"Skype?"

"It's like FaceTime."

"Who are you talking to?"

"That guy in California. The one I met in a young farmer chat group."

"Oh, chat group. Ok. Well, I need you as soon as you finish."

Ben faced the screen again. "My dad," he explained. "I better go." He pulled a red t-shirt over his head.

"Wait!" I yelped, feeling stranded on a half-naked limb. "We had something going there."

"I better not," he said and ended the call before I could show him my best feature.

Over dinner, Mom asked me if I had heard from my "friend".

"I don't know that he's a friend yet," I said. "But, yeah, we had another Skype conversation."

Dad whacked me on the back. "Must've gone pretty well1 I saw the blinds were down!"

I ignored him and directed my attention to my mother. "He's a nice guy."

"When are we going to meet him?" my folks asked simultaneously. Man, were they eager to retire.

"I don't know. We didn't get around to that." My dad smirked.

"Dad, come on."

"When are you seeing him again?" Mom asked, looking daggers at my father. "Do you call it seeing them when it's on the computer?" She looked the question at my father. He shrugged.

"Well, whenever it is, be sure to close the blinds," my father advised and laughed so hard he started coughing.

***

The next time Ben appeared on screen, he was fully clothed. "I can't stay on long," he explained. "I have to drive into Boise to pick up some medicine from the vet."

"Boise? Isn't that in Idaho?"

"Sure is. About an hour away."

"Nothing closer than that?"

"Nope. Nothing. Whole lot of nothing around here."

I told him about my folks' reaction to our first call.

"Jeez. How much did you tell them?"

"Don't worry. I spared them the part about us being half naked."

He looked over his shoulder. "My folks want to meet you," he said.

"Are they there?" I wondered what they thought about my "half naked" comment.

"No, they're in the hall. Can I go get them?"

Before I could answer, he disappeared. When he rematerialized, his face was framed by those of an older man and woman.

"Hello, Dan," the woman said, smiling super sweetly. The man looked grim. "It's so nice to meet you," she continued. The man's frown deepened.

"These are my folks," Ben rather needlessly explained.

"Hello, Mr. and Mrs. Foster."

"Call me Diane."

There was no such offer of familiarity from Ben's dad.

"We're so glad Ben has made a friend so far away," Diane said.

I bet, I thought.

"We like to know who Ben's friends are," Mr. Foster intoned ominously. "So, you're Italian," he said, and not like it was a good thing. Ben and Diane looked nervous.

"Half," was my reply.

A muffled discussion took place. Diane waved and said, "Well, I guess we'll go now. Nice to meet you, Dan. Have a blessed day!" I started to say *and you also*, but Mr. Foster's sour face stopped me cold. The parents left the screen, and Ben reappeared in profile. I heard the door close and catch. He looked at me full face then.

"Sorry," he said glumly.

"No worries."

"They like to know my friends."

"So your father mentioned."

Ben frowned. Guess which parent he looked like. He cast a glance over his shoulder, toward the door. "Look. I'm sorry. I really gotta go."

"Okay. Sure. When should we talk again?"

"Uh, tomorrow's even busier than today. How about Thursday? I'll call you.

The screen went blank. These sudden departures were becoming an irritating trend, but the next day he sent me a video so I forgave him. The shots were full of rolling hills covered in dry grass. "This is where I live," he said in the recording. "I'm out mending fences. We do a lot of that around here. Nothing to do? Go mend fences. See you tomorrow." He gave me a kiss on screen. I assumed his parents weren't anywhere within spyglass range.

The next day, he made his proposal as soon as we finished with the hi's.

"How'd you like it if I came to visit?"

"That would be great! You could fly into SFO or Oakland."

"What's SFO?" he asked. Big internal sigh from me. Good thing he was cute and sexy.

"San Francisco International."

"Oh, okay. Want me to check?"

"After we finish." I actually winked—and I am not a winker. A grin exploded across his face, and he started removing his shirt. This time there was no door banging, parental summons, or any other impediment to our progress.

***

That evening, he texted his success. *Flight 1027 from Boise to Oakland. Arriving 11 a.m. Saturday after next.* I wondered how he talked his parents into it. Maybe it was going to be a surprise. I decided not to do the same for my folks.

"He's flying to Oakland weekend after next."

"We'll go pick him up," Dad said.

"Uh, I was hoping to do that on my own. I haven't met him myself, not in person." *In the flesh yes, in person no.*

"You aren't planning on riding the bike, are you? Where would the boy's luggage go?

"I was hoping I could borrow the Suburban."

"Of course," Mom said, looking at Dad like he better not say no.

"Of course," my father echoed. Then he shook his head. "Son, you really need to get an automobile." He pushed back his chair. "I'll talk with Jésus and Maria. They can fill in for you while your friend is here."

"I can still do the late milking," I said. I was glad to hear I wouldn't have to wake Ben up at 3:30 a.m., the usual time I crawled out of bed for the morning milking.

"How long is—what's this fellow's name again?" Dad asked.

"Ben Foster."

"How long is he staying?"

"Just the weekend. Saturday to Monday morning." *Two nights*, I thought to myself. I started looking forward to both of them. Skype sex only goes so far.

"Be sure to invite him up to the house for dinner and Sunday supper," Mom said.

Dad punched me in the arm—hard—and laughed. "Unless you're having a romantic dinner on your own."

Mom mused. "I guess you'll be going into San Francisco at least one night."

"I guess so."

"He'll probably expect it. We'll plan on breakfasts and Sunday supper," Mom said with a firm nod of her chin.

"Maybe we should buy groceries for just the supper," Dad suggested and punched me in the arm again.

"Dad, I'm getting bruises."

"Oh. Sorry." He patted where he'd pounded.

"Thank you," I said quietly. "For being interested."

My parents looked at each other. "Of course," Mom replied. "We want to see you happy."

"We sure do," Dad agreed. I hugged them both.

***

The flight from Boise arrived in Oakland seventeen minutes late. Those were nervous minutes for me. I went into the men's room three times to check how I looked. When I met him outside security, Ben was equipped with a big grin, a rolling gait, and a backpack. He looked older than on Skype, which was a relief. I had begun to doubt whether he had reached the age of consent.

"Shall we get the rest of your luggage?"

"This is it," he replied. I could have ridden the Honda after all.

He looked up at me and grinned. "You're a tall one." He was five or six inches shorter than I.

"Six-three, like I told you." He grinned again. I whispered into his ear, "If you keep grinning like that, I might have to rip your clothes off and ride you like a pony in the Oakland

International parking lot." He looked alarmed, like he thought I was serious. There was no more grinning until we got in the car and were on the 880 freeway.

I decided to take the long way home, across the Bay Bridge into San Francisco, then across the Golden Gate Bridge and up Highway One. It would be scenic. We drove along the Embarcadero and through the Marina District to the Golden Gate.

"Wow!" he said as we hit midspan. "You can walk across this?" People were.

I agreed you could.

"I'd sure like to do that sometime."

"Why not now?" I turned right into the Marin side parking lot.

Our stroll was sunny but windy. Ben's straight, dark brown hair blew bewitchingly to and fro. I tried to take his hand, but he jerked away and stuffed it into a tight jeans pocket. When we reached midspan again, he stopped, leaned over the railing, and looked at the water flowing resolutely under the great bridge. "Man, that's a long way down. People really jump off this thing?"

I nodded. "Every year."

"You ever see one?"

I tried to ignore the eager look on his face. "No, thank God." I tugged at his elbow. "We better get going. My mom's cooking dinner for us tonight." He looked scared. "They want to meet you." The scared look did not leave his face. "I suppose I could tell her..." What could I tell her at this point? I should have mentioned it to Ben in our daily Skype calls, but we didn't do much talking now.

The color returned to his face. "Naw, it's okay. What's she cooking?"

"Papardelle Bolognese. It's my dad's favorite."

He looked doubtful. "What's that?"

"Sort of like beef stew over pasta."

"Oh. Okay," he said, still looking doubtful.

When we arrived at the dairy farm, I parked the Suburban in my parent's garage. "Wait here," I told him. "I'll just take the keys in the house." But, before I could even open the car door, my father came running out of the house, yelling, "Hello! Welcome!" My mother followed more sedately, merely smiling. I rolled the windows down. Dad extended his hand and nearly all of his face through the open passenger window. "Hello, Ben. I'm Dave Tomasi. This is my wife, Dorothy." Mom wisely kept her hands to herself and just said hello. "Come on in the house," Dad suggested, and opened the passenger door. Ben almost leapt onto the gearbox to get away from him.

"Dad," I said. "I think Ben would like to get settled first." I handed my father the car keys across Ben, which was probably not a good idea since my guest flattened himself against the car seat.

I got out and lifted Ben's backpack off the back seat. "We'll see you at six. Come on, Ben." My parents backed off and Ben summoned the courage to extricate himself from the car and accompany me down the path between patches of produce Maria tended. She and Mom sold the tomatoes, peppers, and squashes at the heretofore mentioned San Rafael Farmers Market.

As we walked, I gave him the lay of the land. I pointed in a southwesterly direction. "That's my place down there." I pointed north. "That's the milking barn. Our hired help's going to take care of the milking, so we can sleep late." Ben flinched. "Anything wrong?"

"No, nothing," he answered, although I think he was sweating.

"Would you like to take a shower, or something?" I asked him when I had closed my front door behind us. He ignored my innuendo and looked around the living room.

"It's nice you have your own place."

"Let me show you the rest of it," I said, trying to take his hand. He jerked it away again, but at least it didn't go in his pocket. Was that progress?

"Okay. Well, here's the kitchen." He scanned it obligingly. "And down this way is the bathroom." He peered inside. "And this is the bedroom." He seemed stuck on the threshold. I pushed past him to put his bag down. "You can hang up your clothes or put them away. I made room in the—"

"Can I have a glass of water?" Ben asked. Before I answered, he headed back down the hall and veered into the kitchen. I followed a little less quickly and arrived to see him seating himself at my third-hand dining table. I filled two mismatched but unchipped glasses with cold water from the refrigerator and took a seat kitty-corner from him.

Ben gulped the water like he had trekked through the Mojave to get to Marin and handed me the empty glass. "Would you like some more?" I asked.

"No, thanks. It was mighty good, though." I set his empty glass down next to my still full one and waited. It seemed like we were on his dime.

"Your folks are really, uh… friendly."

"Yes, they are," I agreed. *Especially my dad*, I thought to myself. I compared my father to Ben's. From the little I knew about Mr. Foster, my dad won hands down.

"How about you show me around your spread?" Ben finally suggested.

I didn't think he meant the one in the bedroom.

"Sure. Do you want to change?" I looked at his neat grey pants, navy sweater, and bright white sneakers.

"Oh, no. I'm fine."

"It can be pretty mucky out there."

"Oh, okay. Maybe I better."

I led the way back to the bedroom and sat on the bed to watch. Ben looked at me like I should leave. I didn't, so he began slowly removing his travel clothes. It was like an unintentional striptease.

"You can hang your shirt and pants in the closet." I got up to get him a couple of hangers.

"Thanks," he mumbled after I hung his shirt up, then his pants.

Skype did not do him justice. "Your body is amazing," I said.

Ben reddened from hair to belly button, ducked his head, and pulled another red t-shirt over it. He seemed to have an unlimited supply. When he bent over to extract a pair of jeans from his backpack, I nearly humped him then and there, but I restrained myself. He turned around, finishing with the zipper.

"I didn't bring any other shoes," he told the floor.

I stood up, hoping my erection was obvious. Ben's gaze followed my legs to my groin. From his raised eyebrows and open mouth, it apparently was, but he looked nervous, so I didn't lunge for him like I wanted to.

"No worries," I said, with only a little catch in my throat. "I've got an old pair. They'll probably fit you." I rummaged in the closet, found the beat-up sneakers, and handed them to Ben. He looked around the room before realizing the only place to sit was on the bed. I decided to let him be and left the room. There would be plenty of time for lunging later on. While I gave Ben room, I put my work clothes on in the mud porch.

We started with the milking barn. Jésus was out herding the cows in with the ATV, and Maria was putting alfalfa out to keep the girls occupied while they were being milked. I introduced my guest and asked Maria if she needed any help. She looked at Ben with an enigmatic smile and shook her head.

The cows began to arrive, bellies full of grass and udders tight with milk. They sorted themselves out at their favorite milking station, inserted their heads through the grate, and began enjoying the alfalfa. While Jésus and Maria went to work attaching milking apparatus to udders, I explained the intricacies of twice daily milking. "But Jésus and Maria are taking care of it while you're here," I assured him. Ben didn't respond. He was intent on the quick application of teat cups to teats. I hoped it was making him a little more interested in me attaching something to him, but after a few minutes, his attention seemed to wander, so I suggested an ATV ride through some of our pastures. There was a secluded rock formation I hoped to make a stop at.

I drove to the first pasture and stopped at the gate, which I unlatched and re-latched after I drove through. At the second gate, Ben volunteered to unlatch and re-latch. At the third, he began to look at his phone. Cow pastures *are* pretty much alike. Once you've seen one—and heard the thrilling details of grasses sown versus natural, there's not much new to learn at the next one. Besides, he had plenty of experience with cattle and grasslands. I drove on.

"See those rocks over there?" I pointed at the outcrop I was heading for.

"Yeah?" Ben said with no evident interest, still scanning his phone.

"Geologists say they're remnants of the Coast Range, the mountains that used to be here." He looked up then but, not seeing any mountains ahead of us, returned to his phone. "What time is it?" I asked. He held up the phone. Five o'clock. Wow, time sure flies when you're not having fun. "We better head back." I turned the ATV toward its shed.

Ben rejected a second offer of a shower and put back on the clothes he had arrived in. I chose a similar outfit. We combed our hair and walked up the hill in time to be greeted at the door by my father. "Your mother's putting dinner on the table," he informed us. That meant no meet-the-parents time before we ate.

Dinner did not go well. The first disaster happened when Dad tried to pour Ben a glass of valpolicella. "Oh, I don't drink," he said. My mother was just bringing in the entrée.

"The ragu is cooked in red wine," I informed him, to save her the trouble. Ben frowned. "The alcohol burns off," I further explained. Ben's frown did not decrease. He looked remarkably like his father. By forty, Ben would have similar lines across his forehead and the bridge of his nose.

"I could make you a turkey sandwich," my mother offered without apparent sarcasm. Ben looked over his left shoulder at her and assumed the phoniest smile I've ever seen.

"Just don't tell my parents," he said, winking. My mother stared a moment before depositing the ragu next to my father, who began scooping helpings onto plates. At the end of the meal, Ben's portion remained in situ, uneaten and untouched.

I helped Mom clear the table while Dad shepherded Ben into the family room. In the kitchen, she set the stack of dirty dishes into the sink with an impressive clatter. "Why didn't you tell me he doesn't drink?"

"Because I didn't know."

"He didn't eat a bite of my dinner. Not even the pasta."

"He ate two helpings of salad," I said.

"Very funny." She grimaced and shooed me away. "Go be with your friend. Heaven knows what your father is telling him."

When I joined Dad and Ben, the topic was cattle ranching. My dad was listening attentively and nodding periodically, while Ben described the Flying F and all that went into running it.

"Mainly we have Herefords, but my brother talked Dad into Charolais. I'd like to run some buffalo, but Dad and Ron don't agree." He seemed a lot more interested in his family business than he had let on during our online conversations. When I sat down next to him on the couch, however, he clammed up. "Oh, I guess I talk too much," he said.

"Not at all," my father assured him as he stood up. "I'll go help in the kitchen," he said and hurried out of the room. He could move pretty fast when he wanted to.

I smiled at Ben. "I'd like to see your ranch sometime." I thought Ben was going to jump out of his skin. "Sometime," I repeated, more to myself than to him. That seemed to seal the deal on our conversation.

"Could you turn the television on?" he asked.

"What would you like to watch?"

"WrestleMania's on."

We still weren't talking when my parents entered the room. Their heads swiveled in unison to the grunting and groping happening on their Sony and back to Ben and me. I clicked the tv off, Mom sat in her chair, and Dad sat in his. They both tried to draw our guest out, but he responded mostly in monosyllables. I began to think it was me. He was gabbing away until I sat down next to him. Maybe if I moved to another chair—no, that's ridiculous. I made a mental note to talk about whatever was bothering him once we were back inside my four walls. I mean, he didn't have any trouble talking to me online. What had I done?

At a decent hour, I suggested we leave. Neither Ben nor my parents objected. As Ben and I walked down the path to my place, I didn't try to take his hand, even though it was dark. Twice burned and all that.

I closed my front door, turned to Ben, and said, "Why don't we talk about this?"

"Talk about what?"

"What have I done to make you so nervous? What can I do to make you feel more welcome?"

"You haven't done anything wrong." He sighed deeply. "Maybe we *should* talk."

I sat on the couch, leaving plenty of room for him. He took the chair, drew in a big breath, exhaled, and began. "I'm a virgin. Weird, right? Twenty-two and still a virgin. You must wonder what you got yourself into."

"I don't think it's weird at all. People come out at different times." *Besides*, I told myself, *you were a fast learner online.*

"I dated women until this year. Didn't have sex with them either. At least, not all the way. I knew what I was."

"And what is that?"

"Queer."

I didn't think Ben meant the word in its current, more positive usage.

"But you do want to have sex with men?"

"Hell, sure I do! Couldn't you tell? I mean, from what we've been doing online?"

"Well, I thought so but, since you've been here, I figured maybe I'd misunderstood."

He came to sit beside me. "You didn't. I want to."

I tried to kiss him, but he looked nervously toward the window. I closed the blinds and returned to the couch. After many kisses and some removal of clothing, I suggested we decamp to the bedroom. Before he could ask, I closed the blinds in there too.

I began again with the preliminaries. Ben and I both reached a second boiling point pretty quickly. "Go ahead," he said solemnly up at me. I wasn't sure what he meant. "Fuck me," he said grimly in clarification.

"We don't have to the first time."

"I want to."

"Are you sure?"

He grit his teeth, pressed his arms rigidly against his sides, and clinched his hands. "Go ahead," he said like a brave soldier and shut his eyes tight. I reached into the night table drawer and pulled out a condom packet. Ben opened one eye. "Why you using that? I can't get pregnant." He tried to laugh, which is hard to do when you're frowning.

"But we can get STDs. And AIDS." Did he know what those were? This wasn't the time to instruct him on sexual hygiene, at least for me. I slid the condom on, lubed it liberally, and pushed his legs back. He yelped in fear. "I'm going to put some lube inside you too," I said. He nodded and clamped his eyes shut again.

His sphincter was as tight as his eyelids but no surprise there. I massaged and lubed, massaged and lubed. Finally, he seemed to relax a little, so I started to ease in. I hadn't gone far when he screamed, "Take it out! God damn, that hurts. Take it out!"

I wondered whether my parents could hear his screams up in the big house and what they thought. Would I hear banging on my door? Would the neighbors call the police? Time would tell. Meanwhile, I whispered, "Just relax, Ben. It'll hurt less if you relax."

"Relax? You're killing me! Get that thing outta me!"

I reluctantly did as he asked. There was plenty else we could do, but Ben scooted away from me and stood up, naked, gorgeous, and now unavailable.

"Could I take a shower?"

I thought to myself, *Oh, now he wants a shower*. "Sure," I said out loud. "Remember, the green towel's mine."

"Got it. Brown towel. Thanks." He ran off to the bathroom, muscles in glorious motion.

I read while Ben showered. Fifty pages later, I heard the bathroom open and put the book down. He stood in the doorframe, with the specified brown towel wrapped around his midsection.

I would have called it seductive if recent experience hadn't taught me better.

"Sorry I took so long," he mumbled, and turned away from me. He pulled a t-shirt down his body and underwear up before dropping the towel. He faced me again.

"I'm sorry. I guess I should have listened to you. About. You know."

I knew.

"It's okay," I told him. "We can just snuggle. There's plenty of time." I pulled the covers back for him, which revealed a few feet of my still naked body.

He swallowed hard. "I guess I'll sleep on the couch."

I waited a long moment before I, like the good host I should but didn't want to be, finally said, "Oh, no. You take the bed. I'll sleep on the couch." I took a blanket from the closet, my pillow, and *The City of Palaces* by Michael Nava with me. I closed the bedroom door behind me and prepared my unexpected bed for the night.

When three-thirty a.m. came, my internal alarm clock went off. I sat up and considered my options. Usually I'd be propelling myself out of bed onto my feet and trudging to the kitchen before beginning the morning milking, but this morning I wasn't alone. I opened the bedroom door carefully and peeked in. Did he always sleep with clenched eyelids or was he just working hard not to see me? Whatever the answers to those questions were, sex clearly wasn't an alternative to milking. I closed the door as quietly as I could, wrapped the blanket more tightly around me against the chill, and padded off to brew some coffee.

After downing a mugful and two pieces of toast, I listened at the bedroom door for any sound of Ben stirring. Hearing none, I dressed on the mud porch with yesterday's muddy, mucky work clothes hanging there and wrote a note to Ben. *Milking the cows. Back by six.* I headed for the cow barn.

Maria was setting up the machines. I could hear the ATV. I set to work distributing the alfalfa. Neither she nor Jésus showed any surprise at seeing me. After the milking was done, I helped Maria clean up while Jésus escorted the ladies back to the pasture. When Maria and I were done, she gathered her gardening tools, murmured "*Adios*, Dan," and left to tend her vegetables. I took the short walk back to my little house. Surely Ben would be up by now. He'd be wanting breakfast, and we needed to discuss our activities for the day.

I could see him from outside and better from the mud porch. He was seated at the kitchen table, dressed for travel. His backpack was by his chair. An empty coffee mug—not mine—sat next to my note. I entered the kitchen, filthy and stinky. I had an inkling he wouldn't care.

He greeted me with, "Could you take me to the airport?"

I looked at him with a mixture of surprise and sympathy. "You sure about this? I mean, let's talk about it."

"I made a mistake."

"I know it's a big step. Coming out—"

"No, sex with men."

"Oh."

"Yeah. I'm sorry. I thought I'd try it."

"You were pretty good online."

"It's different in person."

I couldn't refute that. Maybe an early goodbye was a good idea. "Okay. I'll take a shower and then…"

"There's a plane for Boise in a couple of hours from that Oakland airport."

My hands went to my hips. I leaned forward. I know a few choice phrases in Italian. My mouth opened and shut. I mean, why bother? I stood up straight and put my arms at my sides.

Ben looked a little abashed. A very little. "Sorry. There's not another one until tomorrow."

Heaven forbid he stayed another night under the roof of a Catholic and certified sex maniac. "No problem," I said with as much disgust as I could muster. I returned to the mud porch, removed my milking duds, and headed for the bedroom to don my gay apparel.

"Thanks," Ben called after me. I gave him the finger, but not so he could see.

With hands and face washed and hair combed, I sat on my bed to tie my shoes. I could get the keys to the Suburban, but I'd also have to explain. Mom and Dad would be up. Fuck that. Anyway, mustn't make little Benny late for his return flight. I finished with my shoes, grabbed my leather jacket, keys, and two helmets, and returned to the kitchen.

"Here," I said, thrusting a helmet at him. He looked up at me with questions in his big blues. "We can take the bike."

"Okay. Are you ready?" he asked.

"Oh yeah," I answered. So ready.

I admit to gunning the bike when we took off and going a little faster than I might usually and maybe taking the curves without slowing down as much as the signs advise. Ben held onto the passenger strap all the way and said nary a word. I hoped he was scared shitless.

I left him outside the Southwest terminal. Neither of us said goodbye. I did see him safely into the building before I roared off for home. If he got lost after that, it wouldn't be my fault.

The ride back gave me plenty of time to think. *Maybe it's me. Maybe I'm not meant to be partnered up.* But my angel advocate counter-argued, *That kid's screwed up. Forget him.* I took her advice.

Back in Marin, I took a quick shower and hiked up to my parents'. When I entered the kitchen, they were doing the dishes. "Everything all right, son?" Dad asked. His yellow-gloved hands held a glass plate suspended above the sink.

"Ben left."

"Do you want to talk about it?" Mom asked. Then, with an eyebrow raised, she added, "Or would you rather have breakfast?"

"Breakfast please."

She took the frying pan out of the cupboard, and my dad poured me a cup of coffee.

"Oh," I began, as casually as I could. "Do you still have the number for Helen Zamastil's nephew?"

Mom laughed so hard she collapsed against the counter. She dried her eyes with the dish towel. "I'm sorry, I'm sorry. Yes, I still have it. I'll go get it." My dad stayed with me and, for once, abstained from glib comments. We drank coffee together in silence, which I greatly appreciated. It gave me more time to think. Jeff Zamastil was good looking enough. Nice shoulders. So what if he was a CPA? He had to commute to his office from somewhere. Why not a dairy farm? Besides, he looked pretty hot in a suit. Anyway, his aunt liked him. Maybe I would too. And if I didn't, at least I wouldn't have to cart him back to the airport. He had his own car, after all.

Mom returned with the number. I stuffed it in my back pocket. After eating, I thanked my parents and left. As I walked down the hill, I retrieved the number and punched it in. Maria was hoeing weeds. I waved hello as I listened to Jeff's phone ring. A pleasant male voice answered.

"Jeff Zamastil."

"Hi, Jeff. It's Dan Tomasi."

"Oh, hi. Nice to hear from you!"

I wasn't sure whether to feel relieved, suspicious, or guilty that he knew who I was. "I was wondering…" I began. By the time I reached my house, we had a date for that night. I opened my door and began to clean. I wanted all evidence of Ben to disappear. Not that there was that much. It didn't take long before my four rooms were Zamastil-ready.

The weekend wouldn't be a wash after all. Probably maybe.

Picnic in Moscow

Danger is everywhere. Yes, for a gay man in Russia these days, that is surely true, but it was Friday night and I was tired of hiding in my small apartment. I thought perhaps I could go to a movie. There was a new American film at the Romanov Cinema.

I bought my ticket, entered the theater, and joined others waiting in the café. I hesitated over the menu but finally chose sushi and a celery juice. People around me chatted, laughed, got into political arguments, and ate candy the Romanov doesn't sell. I didn't speak to anyone. I didn't look at anyone. Making eye contact can be dangerous for men like me, men who appear gay.

I am gay, but that is beside the point. It's a matter of looks. I'm tall and slender, with a delicate facial structure. That's the only word for it. Delicate. I have never done drag, but probably I would make a pretty woman. I have clear blue eyes and short, blond hair. Short hair is part of my disguise. Another part is my glasses. I don't need them to see, but a buzz cut and thick black eyeglasses make me ugly. Someone told me the vigilantes don't think ugly men are gay.

I try to avoid attention in other ways too. I wear dark colors and ordinary clothing. Nothing stylish. I would like to buy nice clothes. I could—I make a good salary—but people would notice me, and that would *not* be good. I used to wear clothes that fit and gel my hair. That was before the attacks and killings began. I dream about those days. Will they come again? I don't see how. Russia has never been an enlightened country.

I dream too about emigrating to Germany or maybe France but remind myself that my parents will need someone to help them when they are old. That someone will have to be me, since I am their only child. I have suggested we leave Russia together, but they have parents too—and brothers and sisters, aunts, and uncles. I love all those people but, if my parents were not living, I would not be in Russia now.

At last, the theater doors opened, so the audience before us could leave. I got up with the rest of the people seeing "BlacKkKlansman" but avoided looking too long at anyone, especially the men, most especially the men who looked gay. The vigilantes can trap you with handsome boys.

The attendant accepted my ticket without a word or a smile. The theater is arranged in sofas for two, two sofas to a row. I chose a seat in the first row in hopes no one would join me. The lights were still on, so I scrunched down. It would be safer in the dark once the film had started.

The movie was better than critics said. I think they criticize American movies more because America and Russia are enemies. We might not always be enemies, though. America is just as reactionary as my country under Trump.

I left the theater feeling exhilarated and began my journey home. Back to Tserskaya station, then a transfer to the Sokolnicheskaya line. On the bus, I took a seat up front. If someone attacked me, maybe I could escape out the door. The driver wouldn't help. Probably, she and the other passengers would join in. I looked out the window at grey, blocky buildings with rows of windows lit brightly against the night. I hoped no one thought I was looking at their reflection.

At last, I could signal for my stop. As I stepped down to the street, I unavoidably locked eyes with a young man waiting to board. He smiled, and I smiled back before I could stop myself. Sometimes you cannot help it. Anyway, I thought, *what does it matter?* He is getting on the bus, and the bus is leaving. He was cute though, so he was in my thoughts as I walked quickly toward home and safety. The streets in my district were empty, even though it was a Friday. I could see people inside their homes, watching television or drinking. I thought of my vodka in the freezer. I would have some in celebration. I had had a night out without incident.

I was thinking of the vodka when I heard footsteps behind me. They were hurrying too, so I slowed to let the person pass, but they fell into step beside me. I hoped it was someone I knew.

"*Kak oho*? My name is Vlad," a young voice said. "Like the Impaler." I looked up. It was the boy from the bus. He smirked, alerting me to the double entendre. His face was Russian, not Hungarian--from the dark straight hair to the strong blunt chin. His eyes were wide set and a little slanted. We Russians are more Asian than European.

"Dimitri," I said, reluctantly shaking his hand. It would have been impolite not to do so, and his hand did feel good—strong, warm, and reassuring. He was shorter than I, but most people are. His shoulders were broad inside his short-waisted jacket, and his dark eyes sparkled in the streetlight. His smile was lopsided, as if he couldn't decide whether to be happy or not.

"Do you live near here?" he asked, which renewed my caution. I asked myself why he hadn't gotten on the bus. Why was he following me? I ignored his question and turned again toward home, walking rapidly, but the boy kept pace with me and tried again.

"Is there a place I can buy you a drink?" Even though we were the only people on the street and Vlad spoke softly, I did not think he should say it that way. Usually gay men say, "Is there a bar nearby?" or something like that. We are not making a date, only asking if there is a bar.

In fact, there was a bar across the street, the *Belyy Olen*. I knew the owners and probably most of the people who would be inside. My parents lived two blocks over, in the home I'd grown up in. Moving out was traumatic for them and for me. *It isn't safe for you*, my mother said. She was right, but I was twenty-two and wanted my own life.

Vlad noticed the bar. "Ah, there's one."

He started across the street. I didn't follow but didn't keep walking either. I liked how Vlad looked, and he seemed friendly. *Not everyone hates gay people*, I told myself. At least, not enough to beat me up. I joined Vlad across the street.

Inside, the bartender and several patrons said "*Priyvet*, Dimitri Ilyich" to me.

Vlad seemed impressed. "Everyone knows you here."

"Not everyone," I replied, conscious that eyes were on us. I told him, when he asked, that I would have a Zelyonaya Marka, a less expensive but perfectly acceptable vodka.

"*Nu davayte*," he said. "We can do better than that!" I wondered who was paying when he ordered two double Belugas from Yuliya, the waitress. I went to school with her before university. She knows I like men. She tried to set me up with a cousin, but there was no chemistry.

"But he's a chemistry major!" she said when I told her. I thought that was funny.

Yuliya cut her eyes in Vlad's direction and gave me a thumbs-up. When she returned with our drinks, Vlad and I said "*Spasibo*" at the same time. Also "*Na Zdorovie*" when we clinked glasses. He and I drank and talked about the weather, school, where he lived—Kapotnya, a working-class suburb of Moscow. He was a mechanic. I told him I was a software designer. He seemed impressed.

When he left to use the restroom, Yuliya returned. "He's a cute one," she said. "But be careful, right?"

"Of course."

Yuliya looked at me with her serious eyes, then brought me up to date on her cousin. "He has a partner now. They moved to St. Petersburg." I thought to myself, *Berlin would have been better*. When Vlad returned, she smiled at him, gave me another firm look, and left.

After three drinks each, he asked again if I lived nearby and I said yes. I should not have, but we had been talking for an hour, and I wasn't frightened of him anymore. He was nice and very attractive in a brutish kind of way. He was also careful, which helped me relax. He looked left and right and behind us before he suggested, almost in a whisper, "Maybe we can go there." I thought, *he is like me: gay and afraid. We have found each other, someone to be with.* So, I said we could go to my apartment. It also probably had something to do with the alcohol. In any case, I paid the bill, and we left.

When I had closed the door and set the locks, Vlad took me in his arms and began kissing me. His lips were very full, like mine, and they felt magical. His tongue felt even better. When he started removing his clothing, I did too—enthusiastically.

Vlad embraced me again when we were naked. His lips brushed my ear. "Do you have condoms?" he whispered. I said, "Yes, in the bathroom." "Maybe you should get them." The smirk was back. I left to do as he suggested, looking forward to sex again.

When I returned, he was on his phone. "My mother," he explained, hanging up. I knew how that was. Mine called me several times a day, sometimes even this late. Vlad took me back in his arms, put his hands on my ass, and rubbed himself back and forth against me. In the middle of this, the building buzzer rang. Who would be downstairs at this hour? My parents and friends would call to say they were coming over. It was probably a mistake. I ignored the signal but, without asking me, Vlad buzzed them in and began putting his clothes back on. I heard several heavy footsteps hurrying up the flight of stairs to my apartment. In no time, someone started banging on the door. Several voices yelled. "*Pidor!* Homo! Open up!" Vlad moved to do that, but I grabbed him. He struggled, but I am stronger than people think. I dragged him to the window, opened it, and lunged out. I held on tightly. His body broke my fall.

We landed with a *thunk*. I checked his pulse. He was alive, but unconscious. Men leaned from my window. "Stay where you are! You killed him! We'll get you, pervert!" None of my neighbors looked out to see what was happening. I knew no one would help me. I had to leave, but I was naked! Not even thinking, I removed Vlad's pants and coat, put them on, and ran. Voices behind me yelled, but I did not look back.

As I ran, I thought about where I could go. I didn't want to involve my parents, and I didn't have my phone—or Vlad's, if that was really his name. I heard the thud of it falling next to us on the ground. Yuri Petrovich Alkaev came to mind, probably because he is strong and big, as well as nearby. I made three turns onto more narrow streets and was at his building, ringing his buzzer. What would he think? Would he let me in?

"Who is it?" he asked in a sleepy voice through the intercom.

"Dmitri!" I shouted. The buzzer was loud. I entered the small foyer.

"Dimitri!" he repeated when he opened his door. He looked startled. "What happened?" I flinched when he put his arm around my shoulders and pulled me inside. He guided me to the sofa. "Tell me," he said, making me take a seat beside him. He offered to get me water or a drink, but I didn't want his arms to leave me, so I told him in a rush about the bus and the bar, the phone call, and the window. "You are safe here," he said when the story was done. "We will go tomorrow to your apartment, but now we must call your parents."

"No!" I said, much too loudly. The walls of Yuri's apartment were thin. I could hear the babies next door, which meant the parents could hear me. I made myself speak more quietly. "I mean, not to my apartment." He nodded and began punching numbers into his phone.

"Hello, Ilya Androvich," he said. I was glad it was my father. Yuri handed the phone to me.

I explained to Papa what had happened. I thought he would demand I come to their building immediately, but he merely said, "You are safe with Yuri Petrovich. I will give your kisses to Mama. She will call you in the morning."

I returned the phone to Yuri. "I don't want to go back there," I told him.

"To your parents?"

"No, to my apartment." Although, in truth, I was thinking of both places.

"Shhh," he said. "We will think about it tomorrow." He looked at my clothes. "You are not wearing a shirt. Or shoes!" I explained how I came by what I was wearing, and he looked disgusted. "Let's get rid of these things. You can wear some of mine." Yuri is not as tall as I am and much broader. I didn't think anything of his would fit me, but he wouldn't allow me to wear Vlad's clothes a moment longer. "After what he tried to do to you? No, my friend." He pulled everything off me until I was naked again. Yuri was wearing just a tee shirt and tiny underwear. Everything bulged—except his stomach. Yuri is not a handsome man, but his body is extremely beautiful—and sexy.

You would think, with what I had been through, sex would be the last thing on my mind, but sometimes the mind is not in control. I covered my erection with both hands. Yuri ignored my embarrassment and got up. "Don't worry; I won't molest you. Come, let's get you into some clothes."

His sweatpants and sweatshirt fit better than I expected. Our waist sizes are about the same, and the shirt had shrunk badly. "Krgyz," he muttered as he picked up Vlad's clothes and opened the door to the hallway.

"Where are you going?" I yelped.

Yuri looked back. In three-quarters, he was almost good looking. You almost couldn't see the acne scars that covered his cheeks. Such a strong jaw.

"To throw this filth away."

"Don't leave me," I whined. I hate the sound of my voice when I am afraid or nervous. It gets even higher.

Yuri dropped the clothes inside his door, kicking at them with his thick legs, and came back to me. "Shh, Dmitri Ilyich," he said. "I will do it in the morning. Now, vodka!" He gave me a playful push back toward the sofa.

We sat at opposite ends, drinking and deciding what to do, where I would live, and how to get my things. Yuri did most of the deciding, which was comforting and practical. I couldn't find my mind—between the upset, the late hour, and the vodka.

"You can stay here for a while," he said in a voice surprisingly soft for such a large man. "As long as you like. We will go to your parents' tomorrow and then to your apartment." I started to protest, but he interrupted. "I will be with you, Dmitri Ilyich. No one will hurt you." I looked at Yuri's body. It was massive, yes, but what is one man against many? Still, his confidence made me feel better, so I nodded my agreement.

"Now, we will sleep. You in the bedroom, and me out here." He looked down at me kindly and tousled my hair, then pulled me up like I was a *kukla* and led me into the second room. The bed nearly filled the entire space. Still, it was a bedroom. I had only the one room and was glad I didn't have to share. Yuri Petrovich began to collect the bedding.

"I will sleep on the sofa," I said.

"No, please take the bed."

"I don't want to make you do that."

He smiled. "You are not making me."

"No," I said adamantly and folded my arms across my chest. Yuri's dark eyes observed me for a short while. I wondered what he was thinking.

"*Ladno*," he said. "I will sleep here and so will you.' Perhaps he thought that would scare me into letting him spend the night in the living room. It didn't, so he shrugged and stretched his arms up to remove his shirt. I had seen his body before, but that was in photos. My father shared one with me after I came out of Yuri in a bathing suit. That was five years ago. He looked like a bodybuilder. He still did. I knew Papa was trying to set me up—like Mama did with girls—and I knew Yuri Petrovich, of course. He worked in Papa's office. I did nothing about the photo. I wasn't interested in having a boyfriend at that point, at 18, and certainly not with someone nearly twice my age.

I stood next to the bed, thinking of all this. "I will turn the light out," Yuri said. I suppose he thought I was shy.

When the room was dark, I debated sleeping in Yuri's clothes on top of the bedding, but I knew that would appear strange, so I removed my borrowed shirt and pants, folded them carefully, and placed them deliberately on a small chair wedged into a corner. They joined other clothes already lying there more haphazardly. Yuri led me by the hand to the right side of the bed. When I was settled, he remained standing beside me, looking down. I felt the heat of him and smelled the good scent of a man, something I had almost forgotten.

"Thank you, Yuri Petrovich," I said quietly up to him in the dark.

"You are welcome, Dima. Do you mind if I call you Dima?"

"No, please do." We were going to sleep together; I could let him use my nickname.

"Good," he said, with a happy sound in his voice. "Please call me Yura." I didn't though. Georgie doesn't really suit him.

After a moment more, he said goodnight, walked around the bed to what must be his usual side near the lamp and radio, and slipped in beside me. We didn't touch. I listened to the quiet of the room and Yuri's breathing. I thought about meeting Vlad, our drinking, the feel of his body, the knocks on the door, and the shouts. I wondered if he was badly hurt, if he had died after I ran away.

"You are thinking."

"Yes," I admitted.

"Don't," he said, reaching under the covers for my hand. "I will sing you a song my babushka sang to me when I couldn't sleep." His singing voice was pleasant, though not as deep as I expected from such a large chest. I relaxed and fell asleep.

The next morning, I was in Yuri's arms. He looked as if he were still asleep, so I tried gently to pull away, but his hold tightened, and his eyes opened. "Dima," he said softly, as if he had just noticed me. I waited, not knowing what to say or do. He released me. "You see," he said. "I promised not to molest you." He smiled and brushed my bird's nest hair out of my face.

His phone rang. He answered it and winked. "Nadezhda Kovalenkova. Yes, your son is here." He handed me the phone and rolled off the bed. I spoke to my mother or, rather, listened as I watched Yuri leave the room, clad only in his underwear and t-shirt, and return a few minutes later with two cups of strong, smokey tea. I smiled in gratitude and took small sips while my mother continued to present the dangers of the world to me.

Yuri left the room again, shutting the door considerately behind him. I promised Mama I would consider moving back home and said, yes, I would see her at ten.

After I hung up, I pulled my borrowed clothes back on and tried to comb my disheveled hair with my fingers before I joined Yuri Petrovich in the living room. He patted the sofa beside him.

"And what did mama have to say?" he asked.

"She wants me to move back home."

"Naturally, but you don't want to?" His look was hopeful.

"No."

His look became expectant. "You can stay here for as long as you want, Dimulya," he said, using the name only my mother had called me before. I didn't know what to say. His offer was kind but probably came with strings. But maybe I wanted those strings. In the middle of my thoughts, he stood. "Well, you are probably hungry. I am. I'll make us breakfast before we go to your parents' and then to your apartment." He must have seen the alarm in my eyes because he offered to make the second stop on his own. "Just tell me what you need."

I thought of my clothes, my keys, my wallet, my papers, but who knew if any of those things were still there? I wondered if the gang would be waiting, although an all-night vigil seemed unlikely.

"We will go together," I decided. "First, to my parents to pick up my spare keys and show them I'm still alive..." I laughed, but Yuri didn't. "And then to Soraeyev Street."

After a breakfast of buckwheat and fried eggs, Yuri offered me the shower first. I tried not to use too much hot water. He produced a pair of brown slacks, which fit me reasonably well, and a tan shirt, which did not. While he showered, I mulled over my life once more.

Yuri's hair was curly from the water when he came out of the bathroom. A large brown towel was wrapped around his waist and thighs. His chest seemed even more prominent. I wondered what the rest of him looked like. *You could remove the towel*, I told myself, but felt flummoxed. He observed me for a moment, then asked, "Have you reached any conclusions, my friend?" I shook my head.

He walked to the sofa and stood before me. Had he guessed what I was thinking? Like last night, his presence was powerful, but he smelled now of birch tar and lavender, the soap and shampoo I had also used. *Remove the towel*, I told myself sternly, but Yuri's next words kept my hands on my lap.

"You have four choices, Dima," he said soberly, looking down at me with his sapphire eyes. "Continue living on your own at your current address--" I shook my head vigorously no. "--Live with your parents, live with me, or live with some other friend. All of these can be temporary while you look for another apartment. Or permanent. At least with me and your parents." His smile was very sweet.

I watched his beautiful eyes while he waited. "Thank you, Yuri," was all I could think to say, but I would have to decide soon. Night would come and sleeping arrangements would be required. My body wanted to stay with Yuri, clearly, but my mind had not decided yet.

"I will get dressed," he said and left me alone in the living room.

My mother noticed my clothes but said nothing about them or how I came to be in them. Instead, she announced that we would be going on a picnic. "And of course," she added, "You are invited, too, Yuri Petrovich. We are so grateful to you for helping our son."

My voice whined with my objections. "Mama, Yuri Petrovich and I are going to my apartment to pick up a few things. And besides, it is still cold."

"Your papa and I will go with you to that place. Afterward, we will have our picnic. It isn't that cold, and isn't today some sort of holiday? Yes! Lenin's Birthday!"

"That was three days ago," I pointed out.

My mother waved that fact away as if it were spring mosquitoes. "We will show them," she declared, her mouth tightening. "They can't stop us from enjoying ourselves. Do you still have your packing boxes?"

She nudged my father.

"You cannot stay at that place a moment longer, Dima.," he declared, looking at her. "These people know the address; they may return. Your mother and I want you home with us." Mama nodded and folded her arms across her drooping bosom, ready for a fight.

"Dimitri Ilyich is most welcome to stay with me," Yuri said very quickly and very formally, his chin high, his body almost at attention. My parents looked at each other in surprise, followed by delight in my father's eyes and distrust in my mother's. Yuri looked at me with what seemed like love. I glanced away.

"Where is it to be, Dima?" my father asked gruffly, after another poke in the side from my mother.

I thought of Yuri's eyes and of his body, its muscles and plentiful hair. "Yuri Petrovich's," I answered. Two of them smiled.

My father drove us the few blocks to my apartment. I did not still have my moving boxes, but my mother supplied two large ones and three suitcases. We packed my belongings into them and loaded everything into their UAZ SUV. I remembered our GAZ Volgas and how despondent Papa was when they stopped making them.

I left the key with the concierge, who delayed us by relating what had happened after I escaped. "The police came. I told them you were not at home at the time." She nodded for emphasis. "They wrote it down as a burglary. All those idiots had run away. Even that one," she added, in answer to the question in my eyes.

"Thank you, Galina Rostenkova," I said gratefully. There would be no need to explain, no need to lie about an almost naked stranger on the ground outside my window. We shook hands. I did not ask for the May rent back, which I had already paid.

"Happy Spring! Happy Labor Day!" she called as we walked away.

"*Schastilvogo maya!*" my mother chimed over her shoulder. "A week early, but who cares?" she commented to us *sotto voce*. "The start of spring. Isn't it lovely?" she asked up into a grey and cloudy sky. My father tried to take the heavy box she carried from her. "You have your own!" she exclaimed. "Carry two and have a heart attack. Do you want me to be a widow?"

Yuri and I walked behind them, lugging the suitcases. We smirked at one another as they tussled over the box. When we reached the car, my parents took their places in the front. Yuri and I got into the backseat. I touched the tips of his fingers with the tips of mine. Perhaps no one would see. I looked out the car window at what had been my building. The incident seemed behind me already. My father looked in the rearview mirror at me, eyebrows raised. "Where to, Dima?"

"To Yuri Petrovich's, Papa." I appreciated the chance to reconsider, but I had made my decision. As Yuri said, it might be temporary. My new roommate, or first lover, squeezed my hand, which my mother saw when she turned around after Papa's question. She looked at my father, her eyebrows raised. He shrugged. She settled back into her seat.

"To Yuri Petrovich's," she agreed in her role as navigator. It sounded as if she were making a toast.

After we deposited my things at my new home, Mama announced in a voice that did not invite discussion, "And now the picnic. Stop at that Aachan on Komdiva Orlova. It will have everything we need," she told my father. "Oh, and maybe the Wolkonsky Bakery. They have such good bread."

"And where is this picnic to be?" my father asked as she got into the car.

"Gorky Park, of course," Mama replied, sitting back, purse on her lap, eyes ahead, ready to go. My father sighed deeply. The bakery wasn't really on the way. Still, I knew he would take the detour to make Mama happy. Papa—after sighing a second time—put the car in drive.

"To Gorky Park," he repeated.

I watched my parents talk to each other as my father drove. I saw the nuances of connection, a head leaning, a hand reaching out. They had been together for nearly thirty years. Would people someday look at me and another man and notice the little things that connected us? Would that other man be Yuri? I looked at him beside me. My look made his head turn and his smile grow. He took my hand, and I let him keep it. Maybe, I thought to myself. Why not? *Vremya pokazhet.*

We had bags and bags of food and drink by the time we reached the park. "Let me carry another one," Papa said in vain to Yuri Petrovich.

"No, it's all right, Ilya Androvich," he answered, continuing to follow Mama. "I have them."

My father called out, "Nadya! Stop! Where are you going?"

"To the river," she answered without looking back. Yuri hurried to keep up with her. Papa was exasperated, but he looked at me and shrugged. I shrugged in return. We kept walking side by side.

As Mama laid the picnic out on an old blanket, she apologized. "I am sorry I did not prepare this myself," she said, indicating our lunch. "But, well, anyway, here we are!" I took a *shashlik* skewer from her and eased the onions, peppers, and pork onto my cheerful yellow plate. Mama served us all some *baklazanov*.

"This eggplant salad looks so good," she said, almost smacking her lips.

"It is good, Nadezhda Kovalenkova," Yuri confirmed.

"Here, Yura," my father said, handing him a glass of Bulgarian red wine. My mother's eyebrows shot up at Papa's use of the diminutive, but he stared her down for once.

"Please call me Nadya, Yuri Petrovich. I mean, Yura," she said with an odd look on her face.

Papa winked at me and grinned, as if to say, *my plan succeeded after all*!

Once the fruit and cheese had been served and mostly eaten, I asked, "Yura, would you like to walk to the bridge?" I could not very well continue to call him Yuri at this point. He stood immediately. My parents exchanged glances, Papa's happier than Mama's.

The beach along the river was empty now. I wondered if Yuri—Yura!--and I would be there next month, side by side, in our Speedos and white skin. By then, we might be lovers. Thinking that excited me. Living with him would have certain advantages, I reminded myself.

We reached the bridge. As we leaned over the railing and watched the river flow beneath us, Yura asked, "Do you know where the Moskva goes?" I had never really thought about the river going anywhere. "To the Caspian Sea," he answered, nodding wisely. I did not believe him.

"Really? I didn't think it was that long."

"It isn't, Dima. But the Volga is, and the Moskva joins the Oka, which joins the Volga, so the water we see here," he said, indicating the river below us with his wide hand, "Goes to the Caspian Sea." During his explanation, two men passed by, stared hard at us, and said something to each other.

"I think we should go home, Yuri Petrovich," I said nervously.

"Yura," he reminded me.

"Yura," I agreed. I noticed the men look back at us. That second look was no more friendly than the first.

"And where is home?" he asked, smirking at my discomfort.

"With you," I whispered, looking at him at last.

"I would kiss you, Dima, if I dared," he said.

"Please don't!" I yelped. The two men heard my outburst and stopped at the far side of the bridge. Yura had not noticed them.

He gave me a little push back in the direction of my parents. "Don't worry, Dima. I won't be stupid. Anyway, you have nothing to fear from those two guys. Not with me here." So, he had noticed them after all. He frowned at them, and they quickly walked away. "But I agree: let's go home." I blushed and put my hands in my pockets.

"I am so lucky, Dimulya," he said, blue eyes twinkling at me. The acne scars across his cheeks did not seem so bad now, and his dimpled chin was definitely a positive feature. I wondered how he would look with his hair parted on the right. Yura looked away under my stare. The trees and grass nearby were struggling to grow in the cold. He looked back at me with his usual self-assurance.

"It is a fine day for a picnic after all, don't you think, Dimitri Ilyich?" he said with mock formality. "I always feel more optimistic in spring. New beginnings," he explained, turning serious again.

"Yes, new beginnings," I agreed, but the resonance of that phrase gave me pause.

"You are thinking again," he said, with laughter in his voice.

Was it a sin to think, to have doubts? We were silent together for some moments as we walked back along the asphalt path until we saw my parents ahead, waiting for us on the blanket with the remains of our picnic. My father waved. Yura and I waved back.

My mother called out as we arrived, "A good day for a picnic after all, Dima!"

I nodded my head. Nothing bad had happened to us. Yura had taken care of the two strangers on the bridge with just a look. I began to look forward to returning to my new home and to Yura's bed. Tonight, he and I would sleep there as something more than friends. And tomorrow? *Budem zhit' - uvidim.* We will live—we will see.

Régalos

Our guide led us into yet another formerly grand building full of peeling paint, cracked plaster, and rotting wood, while she talked full speed in her almost perfect English. "This was once the home of the Ministry of …" I raised my hand to interrupt her. This was Tuesday. I didn't want to wait another of our five days in Habana.

"Excuse me," I began in Spanish. "My clients are interested in restoration of the Vedado. When are we scheduled to view that area?"

She looked at her notes. "I do not see that on your itinerary, *Senor* Fernandez."

"Really? I specified my interest in that area in correspondence with Director Mangana. Could I go there on my own?"

Her eyes darted toward our government handler. He spoke up quickly in his calm, reassuring voice. "I will look into that, *senor*. Perhaps, if others are interested…" He looked around the group, several of whom did not speak or understand Spanish. My colleagues looked back, uncomprehending or uncaring. I started to object, but he nodded to the guide. She returned to pointing out architectural details of the former home of the Ministry of Culture. I kept my mouth shut for the remainder of the afternoon. I would give them a few more hours.

We were a group of preservationists from the U.S., Canada, and Europe on an architectural restoration tour of Habana. Essentially, we were in Cuba to see what had been done for tourist dollars. Although I appreciated the important historical work of Eusebio Leal in saving the old city—or at least a portion of it, I represented a coalition of well-off Cuban-Americans from Florida and the New York City area who wanted their grandparents' mansions in the Vedado district repaired, not tourist attractions—and certainly not present or future government buildings.

For the rest of Tuesday, we went on to another building and another and another. By six p.m., I needed a drink—and company of my own kind. I decided to skip the group happy hour at the Kempinski and try a gay bar someone back home had told me about, although Jared's written directions now seemed uncertain in the face of streets without street signs or signs which did not match his directions.

On the way down a *calle* of dilapidated whitewashed buildings, a man was standing under a bruised portico not far ahead of me, smoking. He was also dressed in white, but was much better kept than his building. A tight sleeveless shirt displayed many interesting architectural details. Loose cotton slacks hinted at more. He wore circular framed sunglasses and a noncommittal look. His skin was mahogany dark. As I came near, he said, "*Buenos tardes*," in a tenor voice emanating from a baritone body.

"*Buenos tardes*," I muttered and hurried past. At the corner, I looked up for more imaginary street signs.

"You are looking for something?" he called after me in English.

I shook my head no without turning around.

"What address do you need?" he asked, suddenly at my side.

I answered him in Spanish. "I don't need your help. Thank you." I was not in the market for a *pinguero*, no matter how sexy this one was.

The man looked insulted and abashed at the same time. His face was like a little boy yelled at by his father, even though his body looked like a present for daddy. Against my better judgment, I apologized.

"*Lo siento, senor.*"

"*Esta bien*," he answered, smiling with the beautiful teeth most Cubans have, thanks to excellent state-sponsored dental care. He did not move back to his station under the portico. I didn't move on either. I suppose it was the little boy look or the fact I *was* lost.

"I can't find any street signs," I admitted, with irritation.

"It is confusing, I agree. But you see there?" He pointed at the wall. There was a nameplate. "That is the street sign here." I blushed bright red. "And there?" he continued, pointing at a small obelisk on the ground with a number and an arrow. "That indicates the street number."

"What does the arrow mean?"

"The numbers increase that way."

"Ah, *si si. Gracias*," I said.

He allowed himself to smile now. "*No hay problema, senor.*" He extended his right hand. "Alejandro Munar Rodriguez."

I hesitated, but took his hand, which was softer than I expected. "Miguel Fernandez," I said. My new friend raised an eyebrow at me. I corrected myself. "Miguel Fernandez Rivas." My mother's mother would have been proud.

"I thought you looked Cuban," he said with a wry smile. "Let me guess. Your family left in 1959."

Munar's assumption didn't surprise me. Much of Cuba's upper middle class left after–or before—Fidel Castro took power. My great-grandfather Fernandez was a banker, and *bisabuelo* Rivas owned several restaurants. Under Fidel, neither would have prospered. In America, they did. Eventually.

I nodded yes and got down to it. "Do you know the Cat Club?" I asked. He looked like a man who would.

He seemed to consider the air for a few moments before looking over his shoulder and lowering his voice. "Of course," he replied, followed by more consideration of the air. Then, as if having made a momentous decision, he straightened himself to his full height, which was several inches higher than mine, and said, "It is easier to show you the way than to explain."

"That won't be necessary."

He ignored me, cupped my elbow with his hand, and steered me in the direction I had been coming from. When we reached his doorway, he said, "*Momento*," and ran into the building.

My mouth gaped as the heavy wooden door thudded closed. As the minutes passed, one angel told me to run while another asked how I could walk away from such a body. Before I had decided which one to listen to, my insistent volunteer exited the building. He was now wearing pale blue linen slacks and a lightweight tan sports jacket over his white shirt and brown muscles.

"You look very nice," I told him before I could stop myself. He smiled and took my arm, as friends do in Cuba. We walked together through lefts and rights I knew I wouldn't remember until he stopped us outside a building that looked like all the others—except for a fuchsia pink neon sign above our heads. It proclaimed we had arrived at the Cat Club.

Alejandro followed my gaze to the sign. "It's new," he said. "Well, restored. There weren't any gays after the revolution, and this place went out of business. Things have changed." He looked over his shoulder again. "*Un poco. Después de ti.*" He opened the door for me. We walked into a dark space crowded with men in business suits, dress shirts, summer slacks, and more casual attire, exposing considerable flesh. Some of it should have remained covered.

Munar Rodriguez bought us Cuba Libres, and we sat at an empty table that had magically materialized before our very eyes. We drank our drinks and watched handsome, mainly dark-haired men dancing to Pitbull, Gloria Estefan, and 70s disco on a small, crowded dance floor. "Would you like to dance?" my guide asked. Without an answer, he stood up, removed his jacket, and hung it on his chair. He was back to being the man on the street. "Come on," he encouraged me, sliding the jacket off my shoulders and down my arms. "And you must remove your tie." I did as he said and submitted to him, unbuttoning my dress shirt halfway down my body. "Um," he growled when my chest came into view.

"What about our jackets?"

"No one will harm them," he said and, when we returned, sweating like pigs, I saw his prediction had been correct. I looked around the crowded room, amazed that this was true. Munar Rodriguez winked.

He ordered us another Cuba Libre. We toasted his country. The third drink we toasted mine. The fourth drink we toasted each other. After that, my memory is hazy until the next morning, when sonorous snores woke me in my Cuban government-provided bed. I stared at my bedmate's bounteous shoulders flowing above the cream-colored sheets and his pale lips tight with a dream. I automatically prayed it was not a bad one. I moved to get up, to make us mediocre coffee with the cheap machine my room afforded, but a strong hand gripped my much less muscled shoulder.

"Do not leave me, Miguelito." When had he started calling me Mikey?

"I'm just going to make coffee."

"Later," he said, pulling me back.

After sex and eventual coffee, he announced that he had to rush home. "I must change into my business clothes." Me too, I thought, dreading yet another parade of sagging roofs and discolored walls. "Can I see you tonight?" he asked as he pulled on his slacks. I probably should have said no, but of course I didn't. There was something about his conversation and the feel of his kisses. I had agreed and seen him out the door before I realized he had neither asked for "taxi money" nor requested a gift. If he was a *pinguero*, he was not a very profitable one.

I thought about Alejandro during the day, wondering what he did for work and where he did it. His hands said he worked more with his mind than his body. That he needed to change into something more appropriate for work indicated his job had some weight, perhaps with some responsibilities.

We met outside my hotel, as agreed. He arrived punctually, looking very handsome in his fitted summer blue slacks and tight, pale yellow dress shirt. Straight away, I asked for his cell phone number.

"This is not America," he replied. "I do not have a cell phone." I looked at the flat bulge in his pocket, intrigued that he had lied, but said nothing to contradict him. I wondered whether I should ask for his work number. That seemed presumptuous. I wouldn't do that in the States. He might not be out at work. I did ask at dinner what he did for a living.

"I'm a principal at a secondary school," he informed me. "And also an English teacher." He gave a chuckle.

"Why is that funny?"

He looked at me in disbelief. "You have heard how I speak, no?"

He did have a heavy accent, but his grammar was fine. I assured him his English was perfectly good for teaching others, but he brushed the compliment aside and took up his menu.

"Are there Cuban restaurants in the U.S.?" he asked, changing the topic.

"Of course! All over. You've never been to the States?

"No," he replied, his eyes returning to the menu.

"Not even Miami?"

He put the menu down. "Not even Miami." He hailed our waiter and only after that asked me, "Are you ready?" I selected the fish with Escabeche sauce. He had the national dish, *ropa vieja*.

The *paladar* was a small, comfortable place in Alejandro's neighborhood. Friends and associates kept stopping by our table to say hello and ask about his school, which, it seems, is famous. He introduced me as his American friend. They all seemed to have relatives across the Florida Strait, although nothing closer than cousins or in the same generation. There were numerous mentions, like 'my second cousin Marco' or 'my great aunt Yanet' or 'my grandfather's best friend.'

We had two bottles of good Spanish rioja to wash our meal down. When the bill came, the server hesitated between us. Which to hand it to? I was a rich American, but I was also the guest. Alejandro decided for him. He took the bill.

"Let me pay," I cried, but he shook his head and handed the bowing man cash. I grumbled, "You paid last night as well." His face displayed mock amazement.

"Isn't our government paying for everything while you're here?"

"Yes, but—"

"Then, as a loyal *patriota cubano*, I must pay when you are my guest and prove that communism can also provide capital to its citizens." He said this with a smile and an edge.

"I know the Cuban government provides something to some of its citizens."

"What do you mean?" Alejandro asked, his voice and facial expression at the beginning of anger.

"I have seen some of the houses of your government officials."

He thought for a moment, rearranging his argument. "We may have our own fat cats, but at least we have not elected a fascist as our president."

I had no ready counter for that. I had not voted for Donald Trump, but too many of my family members and associates had.

"No one could accuse Fidel Castro of being a fascist, that's for sure," I said. I sounded like a petulant child, even to myself.

"Do not speak so of Fidel!"

The owner arrived with Alejandro's change. "Gentlemen, *por favor*..." He looked around the room. Our eyes followed his. Yes, people were looking and listening. The man tried to hand the change to me. I shut my mouth and waved the bills and coins in Alejandro's direction. The owner apologized. Alejandro apologized. I apologized. All three of us said, "*De nada.*"

Outside, I asked Alejandro, "Can I get a taxi anywhere near here?"

He took both my arms in his soft, strong hands. "I apologize for discussing politics at the dinner table. I had hoped you would stay with me tonight. I still hope you will." I didn't answer. "May I kiss you?" he asked in a whisper, careful to look on all sides before saying the words.

"Yes," I answered peevishly.

We moved further into the darkness. One kiss was succeeded by several others. There was no further discussion of taxis. Alejandro took my arm, and we were on our way.

"We are here," he said after a few minutes of purposeful walking. He held the door open for me. "It is not the Kempinski, but it has its advantages."

I folded my arms across my chest. "Like what?"

"Better coffee."

I smiled and dropped my arms. Alejandro pulled me across the threshold, and we climbed the stairs to the third floor.

We passed down a quiet hall.

"Does anyone else live here?"

He put a forefinger to his lips. "They are probably in bed already, where I hope we too soon will be."

"Why?" I asked coyly. "Are you tired?"

He opened the door to his apartment, squeezed my ass, and whispered, "No. As you will soon see, *mi amor*. Welcome to my home." I did not take his *mi amor* seriously.

He closed the door behind us. "Would you like a tour or are you weary of viewing decrepit Cuban buildings?"

There was nothing decrepit about Alejandro's three rooms. They were small, yes, but in good repair, tidy, and comfortably—if sparsely—furnished. The bed was a double, and the mattress was firm. I bounced twice. "Comfy," I said in evaluation. Alejandro stood in front of me. I wrapped my arms around his legs and buried my face in his groin. He tousled my hair. I pulled him down beside me. He sent shock waves across the bed when he landed and we toppled over, arms grappling.

"*Mi amor*," he whispered and began to undress me. I let him.

When I was naked, he stood up and looked at me as if he were taking a picture. I held up my arms. He rushed out of his clothing and onto to me. Skin settled onto skin, and an electrical current was completed. Jolts flashed between us. I arched my back in pleasure. All thoughts of politics were gone.

The next morning, over café con leche, we discussed the length of my stay. "Two more days," I said. "Counting today." I didn't say that the final night would be the obligatory goodbye dinner. Who knew if Alejandro and I had even one more night ahead of us? In any case, if I didn't attend the dinner, vindictive bureaucrats might find ways to make sure my clients' goals were never met, even if it meant the loss of personal gain. Already, our government handlers were wounded. I didn't have nightly drinks and dinner with them at our hotel or at other prescribed location in Old Habana. Besides, I wanted to attend the final dinner. Eusebio Leal himself would be speaking to us, making the government's final pitch for reconstruction funds. I couldn't pass up the chance to meet The Man Who Saved Habana.

Alejandro watched me think before saying, "I will cook for you tonight." It wasn't an invitation really, but I accepted anyway.

With a future ahead of us, we showered together and dressed, me in yesterday's rumpled clothes and Alejandro in freshly ironed slacks and a short-sleeved white shirt. The shower had been a tight fit, unlike mine at the Kempinski. Water still glistened among the tight black curls of his hair. I held his face to kiss it.

"I have to leave," I said, trying to convince myself.

"I know," he answered. "But you have not left yet." He embraced me and gave me warm, soft kisses across my face and down my neck, but sex was not repeated. Work loomed for both of us.

We walked close together down the narrow hall and stairway. Morning sounds reached us through his neighbors' closed doors, reassuring me other people did indeed live in the building. Outside, in the sudden sun, he shook my hand and left for his school. No *abrazo*, no kiss. I walked in the other direction toward the Kempinski. Alejandro had marked a map for me.

In the hotel, I hurried into the elevator in hopes of avoiding either my colleagues or our Cuban escorts. I arrived at my junior suite on the fifth floor without incident and surveyed the king-size bed, which was half again as wide as Alejandro's. I opened the louvered door to the small balcony. Somewhere in the city below me, Alejandro was busy with his duties. I wondered if he were thinking of me.

The phone rang. It was Victor, our group's daily government liaison. One might say guard. "I have arranged for a visit this afternoon to the Vedado. It will be a private tour. I will be your guide." He confided this in a low voice, as if he needed to prevent someone else from hearing.

"*Gracias*, Víctor. I am very grateful."

"And in exchange, I hope you will be my guest at dinner tonight."

"*Lo siento mucho*! I have an appointment, I'm afraid."

There was silence at his end of the line. I thought quickly. I had promised dinner and the night to Alejandro. But my clients... so I agreed without enthusiasm and hung up without a goodbye. I thought of Victor for a moment. I had guessed he was gay but had not seen he had any interest in me, at least not any personal interest. What he wanted now, I could assume.

I thought of Alejandro. How could I reach him? What would I say? One of our group seemed to have special contacts within the Cuban government. I would ask her the first question.

For most of the morning tour, I tried to find a way to take Marisol aside, but she was talkative, full of questions and gregarious, always chatting with one or more of our colleagues. Finally, she stopped to refresh her lipstick, lagging behind the group. I lagged as well.

"Marisol, may I speak with you?" I said, behind my hand to her.

She lowered her voice, so it was as quiet as mine. "Of course, Mike. What is it?" I explained that a friend and I had made arrangements to meet for dinner, but my plans had unavoidably changed, and I did not know how to reach him.

"A friend?" she asked, eyes and smile eager. Her face registered the new information she had on me.

"His name is Alejandro Munar Rodriguez. He is the principal of a secondary school."

"You don't know which one?"

I tried not to sigh and limited my words to, "No, unfortunately."

She nodded sagely. "I have a friend…" She blushed at the conjunction of friends. "Someone in the Ministry of Education." She became more flustered. I had to rescue her, or she might withdraw the unmade offer. I suggested an alternate word.

"A contact."

She exhaled gratefully. "Yes, a contact. Shall I check with him?"

"Please."

She winked at me. "I will call him right away." She dropped further behind the group and extracted a phone from her designer purse. I tried not to watch. When she returned, she asked, "Are you ready?" She looked at the bulge in my pocket created by my iPhone, next to another bulge of which I am much prouder. I nodded and took my phone out and in hand.

"Alejandro Munar Rodriguez. Director of the Higher Institute of Technologies and Applied Sciences." She paused. "Mike, I think your friend is someone important." She paused again, her eyes uncharacteristically serious. "And not because he is the principal of one of the best schools in Cuba. My friend asked why I needed the information. He sounded nervous." She hurried on. "I told him I wanted to talk with Mr. Munar Rodriguez about exchange programs with schools in the States."

I resumed breathing. "Thank you so much, Marisol."

She placed her hand on my wrist. "Of course, Mike. But take care, *mijo*. Mr. Munar Rodriguez may want something more from you than--" She stopped abruptly and reddened. "Well, anyway, take care," she finished and bustled back to the front of the group—and to talking, I was perplexed by what she had said but had no time to consider it. I had to cancel dinner with Alejandro. I tapped the number into my phone. I noticed Victor was staring, so I moved slowly forward as the number rang.

"*Buenos dias. La oficina de Director Munar Rodriguez.*"

"Good morning," I answered in Spanish. "May I speak with Director Munar Rodriquez?"

"Who is speaking, please?"

"Miguel Fernandez Rivas."

"Will he know what you are calling about?"

"Yes," I lied.

"One moment please," she said and put me on hold.

Almost instantly, Alejandro picked up the phone. At least someone did. There was a space of dead air, followed by his wary greeting, "Hello, Miguel." I rushed to apologize for calling him at work and to explain. "Of course," he said, his voice relaxing. "I understand. We will see each other after?"

"Yes," I agreed. "I don't know what time."

"*No importa.* Just come. You have your map?"

"*Si. Adios.*" He hung up. I jumped. Victor was standing beside me.

"Anything wrong?" he asked in his perfect American accent.

"*De pinga,*" I replied.

Victor laughed. "You have learned some slang during your visit, *Senor* Fernandez."

I tried to laugh back.

"Shall we rejoin our friends?" he asked and put his hand on the small of my back. The others were nowhere to be seen. "They are in the next room," he explained. I could hear the guide's voice faintly. Victor's handsome tanned face, with its five o'clock shadow at ten in the morning, leaned toward mine. I looked around the room. We were alone.

Victor's laugh was unpleasant. "You look afraid, *senor*. I like that in a man. Come." His hand pressed me into motion and stayed against my back until we reached the threshold to the next room. We were side by side. "After you," he said. As I moved ahead, he muttered something I didn't hear clearly.

"*Como?*"

"Nothing," he answered, smiling with the full wattage of his large, perfect teeth. *Carnivore*, I thought to myself.

The morning passed nervously. Victor smiled like a wolf every time I looked at him, which soon I tried to avoid doing. After lunch with the group in an upscale café near the Museo de la Revolución, Victor followed me to the men's room. "Ready?" he asked my reflection in the mirror. I nodded.

He explained our separate mission to the tour guide, and we left. I glanced at Mirasol. She crossed herself quickly and held up prayerful hands.

Outside, we stopped beside a late model Honda Civic parked half a block away from the café. "My car," he said, with a flourish of his left arm. The car did not look like anything special, but clearly Victor was proud of it. The Civic was dark blue with a grey interior and exceptionally well preserved, as all cars are in la República de Cuba. It had been waxed to a sheen blinding in the mid-day sun.

Victor held the door for me. "*Gracias*," I mumbled as I slid in. He closed the door with a slam. His walk around the car to the driver's side was brisk. A man on an official errand. Nothing personal in this, not at all.

"I have a list," I said when he had shut his door. Victor bent his curly hair over my phone. He looked up at me and grinned.

"So I see," he said, with teeth flashing. "You have even put your e*migrante* mansions in geographic order. Very organized," he sneered. "Well, with such a list, we better get going." The Civic responded immediately to his twist of the key, and off we went, to the tune of "*Loco Contigo*" on the radio.

All day we looked at grand, once beautiful homes, most of which were not in good repair and all of which were occupied, some by my client's relatives as caretakers and others by squatters. The squatters would be evicted.

My inspection of the homes was not comprehensive. The intent was to make a connection, letting the government know how much money my clients offered and what they wanted to spend it on. There would also be—of course—generous contributions to buildings on the government list and to the pockets of cooperating officials.

Halfway through my list, Victor received a call. "*Si*," he said, nodding as if he were talking to a human in person. Then his face froze, his eyes bugged, and his voice turned nervous. "Oh, no, sir! I didn't know this." Silence. "Oh, no, sir!" More silence. "Of course! Of course! Right away!" The hand holding the phone dropped to his side. He looked stricken. I asked if he was all right. He said, "I must make a call. I will be right back." He walked out of the room and far enough away that I couldn't hear this second conversation. When he returned, his face was stony. "I am afraid I cannot keep our appointment for dinner tonight." *Appointment?* I thought. "Shall we continue our tour?" he suggested. No hand on my back or leer on his face this time.

"I must make a call now," I said. Victor agreed without objection. He walked to a dusty window to survey the scene outside, which was full of trees and houses with good bones, but not many people and no bustle.

I punched in Alejandro's office number and was just asking myself, *should I add it to my contacts?* when his secretary answered. "Hello, Mr. Fernandez Rivas," she said cheerfully after I gave her my name. "Just a moment, please. I will put you through."

Alejandro came on the line, said hello, and asked how I was. There was no time lag or suspicion in his voice this time. I told him I could come for dinner after all. He chuckled and said he was glad to hear that. I wondered why he chuckled, but I said I knew he was busy, so I would let him go. I rejoined Victor. His face was full of apprehension.

"Is everything all right, Mr. Fernandez?"

I noted the use of *mister* but only answered, "Yes." The overly self-confident Victor did not return. In his place was a boyish man, eager to please. This boy-man suggested we continue our inspection of the mansion. I agreed.

After speed viewing eleven mansions in the Vedado, Victor dropped me off at the hotel about six p.m., said *buenas noches* politely, and drove off. I was surprised he didn't follow me into the Kempinski. A boy-man can exact sexual payment for services rendered with more unconscious will than a more mature man. I sighed with relief and entered the building.

As I passed through the lobby, someone grabbed my arm. "*Mijo*," Marisol's voice said more quietly than I was accustomed to hearing it. "Everything all right?"

"Yes, he minded his manners." She looked confused. "Victor," I said.

Her confusion cleared. "No, Mike. I meant with, you know, your *friend*." She emphasized the word *sotto voce*.

"I'm seeing him for dinner. He's cooking."

"Oh." She clutched my arm again, her eyes wide with sudden alarm. "You are coming to the farewell dinner tomorrow night, *sí*? The great man himself will be there to address us."

"I would not miss it for anything," I assured her, which was true. Not even for Alejandro Munar Rodriguez and all the coffee in Cuba—at least at this point in the evening.

She hugged my arm and smiled. "*Bueno*! But *mijo*, be careful." I winked. She slapped my shoulder and let me go. "*Besos*," she said in a normal voice and blew me one as I walked away.

Upstairs in my room, I showered, changed, and hurried downstairs and out of the building. I followed my map to Alejandro's door. He buzzed me in, and I climbed the staircase to his floor for the first time on my own. My steps exploded on the bare wood; the sound echoed all around me. Television, music, and conversations accompanied me down his hallway. I did not have to knock; he was waiting for me, framed by an open door. He greeted me with an *abrazo* but no *beso* until he had closed the door behind us. The intriguing smells of home cooking lured me into the kitchen after him. He opened the oven door, which allowed aromas of *lechón asado* to flood the room. He closed the oven, took up a knife, and began slicing plantains. He cocked his head at me.

"How was your day, Miguelito? Did you find any of our buildings you can save?" His expression was not flippant, although the question might have been.

"Yes," I replied. "Many. My clients will be happy."

"They should be. But the poor people living in these homes will be more than sad when they are evicted from your *clientes'* mansions."

I withdrew a step from him. "How did you know what I was looking at today?"

"You told me."

"I didn't."

He put the knife down and pulled me to him with the strength I knew he had. He kissed me on each check, the mouth, and neck and then resumed slicing the plantains. "I hope there is enough money," he said without looking up.

"There is," I replied.

An arched eyebrow emphasized his doubtful stare. "There is never enough money," he said in a flat voice before resuming his slicing. I decided to move on.

"Can I help?"

"No, but thank you for offering. Everything is almost ready. I just have to fry the *tostones*. Pour yourself some wine. It's Cuban, from the Camaguey."

I looked at the label. "I have a friend whose family is from this area."

"It was my home," he said, his back now to me. "Perhaps my family worked for them."

I ignored the implication. "They owned a store."

"My family worked in the cane fields."

"What's Camaguey like?" I said, to avoid any renewed discussion of communism versus capitalism.

He lifted the lid of a pot that smelled like beans and another that was rice. "Agricultural. Very beautiful. The countryside and the city," he said while he poured oil into a skillet. I watched him drop the slices of plantain into the pan and begin to push them around and flip them over. I had seen my *abuela*, my mother, and my aunts do this many times.

"It all smells so good."

"It will taste good, too. Now let me serve the food before it gets cold. You will like this, I hope. Very traditional. *Lechón asado, tostones, y congri.*"

He mixed the rice and beans in a serving bowl, and placed helpings of everything on large blue, yellow, and white patterned plates. Once he was seated, he took up his stemless wine glass and toasted me with, "*Salud, por que el bello sobro*!" It amused me how he changed the traditional toast to a woman's beauty to one of a man's.

"*Gracias*, Alejandro. That is very kind of you."

"*De nada*, Miguelito." He took a bite of pork, chewed, and swallowed. His eyes prepared a question. "I was wondering..."

"Yes," I encouraged him.

"Why is it that you have not visited your own family's mansions?"

"How do you know I haven't?"

He ignored the question. "Would you like to? I can arrange it."

I did wonder how a school principal could manage this, but remembered Marisol's words and simply answered, "That would be nice."

"You do not have to continue the daily group tour tomorrow," he said. My eyes must have shown the surprise I felt because he quickly added, with a wry smile, "I mean, now that your mission is complete."

I drank some wine. "Step two is complete, but my mission is not. The government has to agree my project can proceed."

"I am sure there will be no problem with that," he said before he put another bite of *lechón asado* in his mouth.

I put down my utensils. "How can you be?" Was Alejandro Munar Rodriguez important enough to make sure my clients' wishes were granted? He took a forkful of *congri*, chewed, and swallowed while I considered my options. I could leave or I could eat. Or keep talking. "I would have to get permission," I ventured. I watched his eyes. They told me nothing.

"That would also not be a problem. I have to be at the school until early afternoon. I can meet you at your hotel at two." I said that would be fine. That settled, he went on to another topic. "How do you like the pork?" he asked.

"*Mis felicitaciones al chef*," I answered and returned to eating.

After dinner, Alejandro played Cuban music—traditional *danzon* and more recent *reggaeton*. We danced close to "Lo Aprendió Conmigó." It told a sad story, but I liked the beat.

"I love this one," I said.

"Do you know the words?" he whispered into my ear as he bit my earlobe.

"Of course," I answered and sang along with the vocal.

"Do you have someone back in New York who would be jealous?" he asked. He pulled away to look for my answer, but kept his hands on my waist.

"Did I tell you I live in New York?" He didn't respond. "Anyway, no. There is no one."

"Come," he whispered, and led me to the bedroom.

In the morning we continued our now routine, showering together and sharing coffee and toast *con leche* before we headed out for our separate days. I tried to tell him I had the farewell dinner that evening, but he seemed not to hear. He sniffed me like a dog in heat after our shower and pinched my ass before we exited his apartment. "*Ay, mijo*," he said as he held the door for me. On the street, it was sunglasses on and a curt "*Adios*" before he walked away without looking back. Nothing further was said about this being our last day.

I decided not to forgo my morning's obligation to look at rundown office buildings from the 1920s, just in case Alejandro could not deliver on his promises. It didn't matter to me whether the Office of the City Historian or my lover told me the price my clients had to pay. *Lover*, I thought to myself. That he was. Strong and directive, but also gentle and considerate.

"*Ay, mijo*," a woman's voice whispered in my ear. "You are thinking of something nice, *no?*"

"Marisol. Uh, I *was* daydreaming a little."

She elbowed me gently in the side. "Sweet dreams, for sure." She winked at me and returned her attention to the droning of our guide.

After our group lunch near the Kempinski, she suggested we take a walk, so she could hear the details of my daydream. "But not too explicit, Mike. I am a gentle flower." We both laughed at that. I pulled away from her encircling arm. "Unfortunately, I can't. I am meeting someone."

Her eyebrows raised. "Another private tour?" She looked around for Victor, who was chatting with a thirtyish woman from Miami. "He didn't make you do this, did he? I never trusted him."

"It's not Victor."

She looked even more alarmed. "Not—him?"

"His name is Alejandro."

"I know *that,*" she complained.

"He's taking me to see my family homes."

"You could have asked the government to do this."

"I think he is the government."

That took her aback for a moment before she rushed to say, "I want you to call me the minute you get back in the hotel."

My phone buzzed. A message from Victor. Alejandro was waiting outside the restaurant. "I have to go."

"Call me!" she said to my retreating back. I raised a hand, whether in agreement or dismissal, I would leave to her imagination.

Alejandro and I greeted one another with a formal handshake in front of who knows how many pairs of inquisitive eyes. "How did you know where I'd be?" I asked, trying not to look over my shoulder.

He grinned. "Come see my car."

I followed Alejandro, and the eyes followed me to a classic Corvette convertible parked in a no-parking zone. The car was red with a white swoosh along each side and white sidewalls on each tire. In perfect condition, as far as I could see.

"Beautiful."

"1959," Alejandro noted. What I really wanted to know was how could he afford this on a teacher's salary. Maybe principals made more money. A lot more.

"I hate to blow all those curls around," he said, looking at my hair.

I should have taken time for a haircut before I left, I told myself. To him, I said, "My hair will survive." With that pert comment, I opened the passenger door and got in. Back at the outside tables, my group occupied, excited conversations in English and Spanish broke out.

Alejandro slid into the driver's seat, started the engine, and saluted in the direction of the restaurant. Several mouths fell silent and open; others laughed. He eased out of the no parking space, looked carefully behind us, and roared off into traffic.

"Where are we going?"

"First stop is your mother's."

"It's not my mother's. Her family's. I let my cousins know we were coming."

He turned to me with a look I can only call suspicious. "You keep in touch with people here?"

I shook my head. "Not me. An aunt. My mother asked her for their contact information." From his bland expression, I wasn't sure how my admission registered with him. Was he appeased or just filing the information for further investigation? Whatever, he drove on, looking at the road ahead.

We entered the Vedado, an area of homes and small businesses. Alejandro recognized the house before I did, although my Aunt Marisa had emailed me several photos of it and of the cousins who lived there. "There it is," he said, "And a parking space." A good-looking young man was standing in the space, which was centered in front of the short lawn leading to the building. He was easily recognizable as part of my mother's family. In fact, he was a taller version of me. I'm often told I look like my mother.

Alejandro noticed. "Your cousin?" I nodded and waved. The young man waved back and stepped out of the space so we could park. He opened the passenger door for me once the Corvette was still.

"Welcome, Cousin Michael!" he said in a decent American English accent. We shook hands, but he pulled me to him in an *abrazo*. He smelled of lime and cedar and felt warm and solid.

"Thank you…"

He gave a chuckle. "Conrado. We are third cousins, I think." He chuckled again. "I am never sure of these things. We can ask Mama." He looked at Alejandro and his warm smile turned cold immediately. I introduced them.

"Alejandro Munar Rodriguez. My cousin Conrado."

"Conrado Colon Rivas," my cousin said with ice in the words. He pointedly kept his hands at his sides. Alejandro looked like he recognized the name. From the stare he gave Conrado, I doubted it was because my cousin and I shared a maternal surname. He dropped his hand.

Before the standoff could get too tense, an explosion of people erupted from the house, which was really a mansion. They spilled through the six porch pillars, adults clattering down the wide entrance steps and kids jumping over multi-colored flower beds full of roses onto the immaculate lawn.

"My family," Conrado explained. He winked at me and corrected himself. "Our family. They are anxious to meet you." In a moment, I was surrounded by shouting, smiling people, many of whom looked like my *abuelo* Rivas, my mother, and her siblings. Hands reached out for my shoulder, my back, and in one case, my ass. I jerked my head around to see Conrado smirking. Repeated kisses wet both my cheeks. I was embraced until my ribs almost cracked. Finally, a tall woman who looked very much like my Aunt Marisa called everyone to order in Spanish.

"Give him space, my friends! Let him breathe!" To me, she said in English, "Welcome, Michael. I am your cousin Elena. We are so glad you are here. Come in, come in." I looked around for Alejandro. He was standing apart, speaking with an older man. He worked his way through my relatives to me. My aunt nodded—not very graciously, I thought—when I introduced him. "Your friend is welcome, too," she said with an arch in the words and in an eyebrow. After that, she turned on her heel and walked purposely back toward the house. Alejandro, I, and the crowd followed her up the flagstone path, onto the porch, and into the yellow and white home my mother's father had lived in as a boy.

The brief central hallway led to a staircase in the middle and open doorways on either side. Its walls were painted a paler yellow than the exterior and lined with art, traditional and modern. I began to feel the spirit of my grandfather, looking through my eyes at the home he hadn't seen again after 1960. Elena noticed the tears in my eyes and pulled me close.

"You are always welcome here, Michael," she whispered to me in Spanish. "This is your home, too." I wiped my eyes and thanked her. She let me go. "Conrado, will you show your cousin the house?" Conrado stepped up immediately to perform this duty.

"With pleasure, Mama."

I looked around for Alejandro. He was chatting with some of my relatives but smiled and gave me a sign I should go on my own, a nod of his head to the side.

Conrado observed this exchange and asked me, with his eyes still on Alejandro, how I knew him.

"He's a friend."

"A friend," Conrado echoed. "How long have you two known each other?"

"Just a few days," I admitted, and hoped I wasn't blushing.

Conrado gave me a lengthy, impassive look, then smiled, slipped his arm through mine, and led me into the room on the right, a formal parlor. We progressed counterclockwise into a dining room lined with rich brown mahogany paneling, then into a kitchen busy with more women who looked like my mother—all marshalled by Elena. From there, we entered the hallway again. Open double doors on our right gave a glimpse of another porch and an elegant fountain burbling in the middle of a sizable backyard. I saw graceful trees, colorful flowering bushes, and bits of another perfect lawn. Across the hallway, we entered a family room, a library, and sitting room at the front. Along the way, I met more cousins—all of whom embraced and kissed me—before we arrived at the foyer again.

"Would you like to see the bedrooms?" Conrado asked, eyeing the stairs.

"How many are there?"

"Six."

I fanned myself. "I think I'm too exhausted."

"Not even mine?" he asked with another wink.

I considered for a moment what it would be like to have sex with someone who looked so much like myself—but just for a moment. I shook my head. "Not even yours, cousin."

Conrado laughed in delight. "Let us find your *friend,* then." I wasn't sure the emphasis he put on *friend* was positive or negative.

Alejandro was in the righthand parlor, a drink now in hand, listening patiently to an older man. The man was badly stooped;

Alejandro had bent to hear him. He raised his eyebrows when he saw me and looked from me to Conrado, who gave him a derisive salute. Alejandro straightened to his full height immediately.

"I will get you a drink," Conrado said to me. "Wine or maybe a mojito?"

"Mojito, please."

Off he went, and I joined Alejandro. He seemed lost in thought, looking over the top of my head at something.

"Should we go?" I asked.

"No. There is no hurry. Enjoy yourself." He paused, weighing his next words. "What do you know about your cousin?"

I looked around. "Conrado?" Alejandro nodded. "Nothing," I answered. "We just met. Why?"

"Nothing," he echoed with a disbelieving frown. I looked again for Conrado, as if seeing him would tell me what was going on. He was returning with two drinks in hand. Nothing about the image told me anything other than I had made the right choice not to go upstairs. The manful stride of my cousin's powerful legs and the activity between them told me that.

Conrado handed a drink to me and held the other out to Alejandro. "I thought you might need another."

"*Gracias, camarado*," Alejandro replied. "But please keep it for yourself. I have a little left." He held up his half-full glass, then leaned back a little. "You know, you two look remarkably alike." I blushed, but Conrado returned the comment with a grim smile.

"Twins separated at birth," he replied, with no humor in the words.

I was feeling the foreigner in this exchange and a little lost. Conrado put his arm around my shoulders and sipped his drink. He and Alejandro stared combatively at each other over crystal glasses. I left them to it to meet other cousins. I figured one or both of them would eventually explain.

I had a long conversation with *Tia* Elena—I could not call her cousin, took a plethora of photos of people, the house, and yard to share with the American family, and received many phone numbers and email addresses. I was having too much fun to keep track of time, so I flinched when Alejandro whispered, "I'm sorry *hermoso* but we really should leave now. You have another family home to see." His breath was hot against my neck.

Expressions of joy and sadness followed us to the car. Conrado opened my door for me and said into my ear, "Such a nice automobile for a schoolteacher."

"How do you know he's a teacher?" I whispered back.

"I will text you," he promised. I wanted to ask what else he knew, but Alejandro started the car, and off we drove off to waves, honks, and many shouts of *vaya con dios*.

When we entered the Miramar district, I began to have an inkling my other great-grandfather's house might be something grander than the big yellow one we had just left. I didn't know anything about it. My father's family never spoke of Cuba or shared photos—if there were any. My *abuelo* and *abuela mayor* Fernandez had left the island with little more than the clothes on their back. I assumed they had to flee, but didn't know. My *abuelo* and *gran tio* and *tias* were too young to remember very much. I did know the family had been very wealthy, the owners of a network of banks in Habana, Santiago, and other large cities across Cuba. In the U.S., my *bisabuelo* became a loan officer in a bank in Union City, one with many Cuban customers. He was quickly promoted to branch manager, then vice president. At last, he promoted himself to owner of his own bank again, one that catered to the Cuban expat community. His son and grandson expanded Nuevo Banco Fernandez into several branches in communities along the East Coast until it was bought by Citibank. Dad became a member of the board of directors.

We parked in front of a high fence made of thick metal stakes and thinner crossbars. A huge white building presented itself in pieces through this enclosure. Alejandro asked, "Are you ready?" I peered through the fence again. The house did not look like it welcomed our visit, but I said yes and got out of the car to face the rest of my past.

An open gate eight feet tall allowed us entry into a paved driveway. I halted a few steps inside to view the building without obstruction. It was a more modern, much more expansive two-story mansion than my cousins' home in the Vedado. I couldn't tell which decade it was built in or in what architectural style. It lacked identifying details. A central cylindrical tower thrust skyward, flanked by two-story wings jutting ominously horizontal on either side. Further one-story symmetrical extensions of these wings appeared squashed by the weight of the remainder of the edifice. It was not a happy construction, as my design professor would say.

"There was some damage," Alejandro said to my unasked question. In the revolution, I assumed. Had some of my father's family died here? Is that why this place was never spoken of? If my surviving family knew, would they tell me? I faced the building, wondering.

"Would you like to look inside?" Alejandro asked. He took my elbow and pulled me forward, so there was no need for a response.

Between gate and house, the lawn was extensive, freshly mowed, and devoid of plants, except for an arrangement of non-flowering shrubs in the circle the driveway looped around. The building loomed more oppressively the closer we got. The wooden front doors were dark with age but swung open easily after Alejandro used a key and pulled the brass vertical handle, which was shiny as new.

We entered a grand central hall the full height of the building. Light flooded down on us from the glass ceiling above. A wide staircase of white marble mottled in pale grey led to a mezzanine that circled the second floor, even past the series of tall front windows above the main door. Single doors on the second floor—all closed—led to the west and east wings and to the rest of the central portion. I wondered what secrets lay behind them, but something whispered not to ask.

"This building," he informed me as my tour guide, "Until recently housed government offices."

"Which department?"

He ignored my question. "Let me show you the rest of the rooms."

We progressed from the marble floors of the atrium to intricate parquet in some downstairs rooms and plain wooden floors laid out in long strips of oak in others. All the walls were white and bare. The woodwork around the windows was painted a glossy black, which added to the institutional feel. It was as if no one had ever lived here, but people had, my people.

"Would you like to see the second floor?"

"Does it look like this?"

"Yes. Basically."

I had passed up my chance to see the second floor in the Vedado, for good reason. I pivoted in place, taking in the mezzanine of this building for a second time. Once I faced Alejandro again, I replied, "No, *gracias*." He seemed disappointed. "If it means something to you…" I began.

He brushed the offer aside. "It means nothing to me, my friend." He observed me for a moment. "Do you know the history of this building?" he asked.

"I know nothing about it."

He nodded and began the story. "It was built in 1946 by Miguel Fernandez Fuentes for his son Miguel Fernandez Alcantes." Miguel Fernandez Alcantes was my great-grandfather. "It was a wedding present. Fernandez Fuentes lived in the ancestral home elsewhere in the Miramar." He paused. When I said nothing, he added, "It is now the Bulgarian embassy."

"Oh." I wondered if I had seen it. Our tour bus had passed many embassies. I didn't remember the guide identifying any of them as Bulgarian.

"You said this place was damaged. What happened here?" He ignored my question.

"Shall we look outside? There are benches and a swimming pool in the back. We could sit. It's quite peaceful."

I thought to myself, *now it is.* I wondered if I had any paternal cousins left in Habana—or in Cuba, for that matter. Only distant, I imagined. Did they have any connection to this place? I doubted it.

There was nothing of interest to me here—personal or professional. I shook my head in answer to his question.

"Are you sure?"

I closed my eyes and let the question settle inside me. Within moments, faraway gunfire echoed in my mind. Unseen hands touched my arms and caressed my face, kindly voices whispered into my ear. My ancestors had come. I felt them all around me—and other spirits, not as loving. *Leave*, they all told me, *and quickly*.

Alejandro caught up with me on the lawn. He peered into my face. "Are you alright??"

I looked back at the building. Pale figures seemed to peer from the windows. Their hands waved me away.

"It's a pity. I had —hoped…" He stopped himself. "You were so happy to see your maternal family's home."

I turned toward the street and regained self-control. "There was life there," I said in a resolved voice. "There isn't any here." *Only death*, I said to myself.

"Yes," he mused, looking back at the building. "I see what you mean."

We began to walk toward the car. On the sidewalk he said, "Just let me lock the gate." I waited impatiently, shifting my weight from foot to foot. It was getting late. I had to prepare for the final banquet. I felt in need of a thorough bath.

He drove back to the hotel but did not get out of the car with me, did not even turn off the engine. "Tonight is your farewell dinner," he said, keeping me beside the car. He had heard me, after all.

"Yes, the Ministry of Tourism is hosting it. I have to go." I thought he would suggest we meet afterward or offer to take me to the airport. I had my *no* ready.

"I will see you tonight then," he said unexpectedly.

"Tonight?" I repeated stupidly.

"*Sí.* At your dinner."

With that revelation, he accelerated away. I watched the car merge into traffic. It stood out quite a while. He would be at the dinner. Why? How? I asked those questions more than once while I prepared myself for the evening festivities. I wore my best suit and newest tie.

"You look very nice, *mijo*," Marisol said.

"So do you. That dress is the perfect shade of pink for you."

She smiled semi-modestly, then asked, "What table are you sitting at?"

"One."

"Oh!" she exclaimed delightedly. "So am I. With my friend from the Ministry of Education and--" My phone buzzed. The promised text from Conrado.

"Excuse me. My cousin," I explained. I scanned the short message.

He is G2. Secret police.

At that moment, a familiar hand—soft and strong—gripped my shoulder. Marisol's eyes widened in surprise—or fear. I wasn't sure which. I turned to face Alejandro. He embraced me. Marisol recovered quickly.

"*Senor*, I am surprised to see you." She looked at me. "Mike hadn't told me."

"Alejandro Munar Rodriguez," he said, placing his arms at his sides and bowing slightly to Marisol.

"Oh, I'm so sorry. I thought you knew—"

Marisol interrupted me. She smiled coquettishly with her mouth and looked daggers with her eyes. "Marisol Vargas," she said, deliberately omitting her mother's surname, which she normally used, at least in Cuba. "I know of you, of course, *senor.*" She paused. Her smile became grim. "Perhaps you have heard of my grandfather, General Manfredo Vargas de Villera?"

Whatever Marisol meant by her words, Alejandro met the challenge. His smile returned, as grim as hers. "Of course. A most worthy opponent for President Castro."

Marisol opened her mouth to say something in response, which I could not think how to interrupt, when someone said into the microphone at the dais, "Ladies and gentlemen, comrades, please take your seats. Dinner is served." Alejandro and Marisol led the way to a table in the row nearest the dignitaries. I could see how frail Eusebio Leal was. He was almost as grey as his suit, which appeared to be badly pressed. The wrinkles in the jacket and pants mirrored those in his face. How he looked was sad news for me. He was the key that opened the door to Cuba for us, and I was grateful. But gratitude faded as Alejandro spoke in my ear. "Quite a good table we have."

"I can see every flaw," I said. He raised an eyebrow. "In the faces on the dais."

"Yes, every wrinkle," he agreed, staring hard in the direction of Leal.

After we had seated ourselves, a tall, slender gentleman, silver-haired and dark-suited, joined us, kissed Marisol on both cheeks, and sat in the empty chair beside her. They faced Alejandro and me across the table. Two other members of our architectural tour group intervened on either side. They were the most prominent among us, heads of major architectural firms in New York and Miami. Marisol leaned forward. "May I introduce my friend, Octavio Fuentes De Guerra, his honor, the Deputy Minister of Education?" We all introduced ourselves in turn. When Alejandro spoke his name, Fuentes De Guerra blanched slightly.

Dinner began with *frituras, broquetas,* and conversation, nervous between some of us, intrigued by others. "Leal doesn't look well, does he?" Marco Naranjo observed over the *churrasco estilo.* He was the head of Naranjo, Serrano, and Jones in New York.

"Well, after all, he is in his seventies," Franco Menendez of Architectural Design Miami put in. Both of them looked to be in the same age category as Leal.

After the *arroz con leche,* the mistress of ceremonies called us to order. She was from the Ministry of Tourism. We had met the first day, but I didn't remember her name. She went on with her welcome without re-introducing herself. "Thank you," she began, "to our North American and European friends. We have been honored by your presence. All Cubans hope—and believe—your visit will be of benefit to you—and to Cuba." She swept her arm across the room to enthusiastic applause, which changed her generic smile to a gratified look. She waited for the clapping to subside, then continued. "Let me introduce our guests at the head table. Although," she added with a manufactured chuckle, "they probably need no introduction." Polite laughter followed before she went through two-minute resumes for a general, her boss from tourism, and a political figure. At last, she arrived at Eusebio Leal.

"And now, ladies and gentlemen, the savior of Old Habana, our city historian, *Senor* Eusebio Leal Spengler!" I noticed Alejandro frown at these words and at the ovation the name received. Everyone in the room rose to their feet, as if pulled by the same string, including—belatedly—Alejandro. Applause rocketed off the walls of the ballroom. Shouts of "*Viva, Leal*!" and "*Gracias, Eusebio*!" erupted in bursts across the room.

Our MC spoke close to Leal's ear, and he rose to his feet with a struggle and the helping arm of the general, who was seated next to him. He tottered to the microphone two steps away—which he turned into three, braced himself with both hands on the podium, and leaned toward the mic. He spoke eloquently and at length in a surprisingly strong voice of the value to the world of preserving Cuba's architectural heritage, of what had been done and what still needed doing. He deserved his reputation; his words were inspiring and memorable. "The buildings are not at fault for the sins of our ancestors" and "We must remind ourselves of where we have been to know where we are and to decide where we should go" are some that still ring in my memory.

Afterward, those on the dais mingled with those of us at the tables below. When I was introduced to *Senor* Leal, took both his hands and gushed, "Sir, you have done so much for architecture, for Cuba!"

"Yes," Alejandro interjected. "For Cuba."

Leal stiffly turned his head in Alejandro's direction. "Ah, c*ommandante*. Was I being recorded?"

Alejandro's smile became more forced, but he did not answer.

At the end of the evening, which was signaled by Leal's departure, Marisol came to me with a whisper, "I have learned more about your friend."

I whispered back, "I have as well."

"G2?"

I nodded.

She looked nervously at Alejandro, who was chatting with the general and the political representative across the room from us. "What does he want with us?" Her eyes darted to me. "Why is he here tonight?"

"Because of me," I replied, wondering if that was true.

Alejandro began to make his way to us. Marisol said resolutely, "I will not leave you alone with that man." I pointed out that I had been alone with him for several nights and many hours already. "Still," she sniffed and refused to go.

Alejandro bowed and nearly clicked his heels at her. "*Senora.*" He turned to me. "Shall we go?"

Marisol threaded her arm through mine and pulled me close. "Mike is staying in the hotel tonight. We have a very early plane. As I'm sure you know," she could not stop herself from adding.

"I will drive *Senor* Fernandez Rivas to the airport myself," he answered with an amused look. "I have a very fast car."

Marisol began to object. I interrupted her. "Marisol, I need to speak with… the *commandante* alone for a moment."

"But Mike!—"

"Please, my friend."

She stared into my eyes, sighed, and withdrew her arm from mine. "I will leave my cell phone on all night. And keep it charged!" she said, nearly spitting at Alejandro's feet.

"So, you know?" Alejandro asked without expression, physical or verbal. "I am not really a *commandante*. At least, that is not my official title."

"I know you are G2."

"Yes, I am a member of the Dirección de Inteligencia, but that has nothing to do with us."

"You just happened to be in my path?"

He looked exasperated. "You know I was standing outside my home, smoking." I crossed my arms in defiance of the truth. His eyes flashed. "Miguel, I assure you it is not among my duties to accost wandering architects."

"Even American ones of Cuban émigré heritage?"

His eyes went dark, and his face tightened. "You were a pretty thing lost in Habana. I could not help but speak to you. And then…" He stopped himself, squared his shoulders, and raised his chin. "You were a diversion. Nothing more." He looked behind him. Marisol was there, too obviously not listening. "*Senora*, the information I gave you earlier was incorrect. Your friend is staying in the hotel tonight." He bowed to both of us, did a military-grade about face, and exited the room in long, liquid strides. I could not help but admire how well his body moved in his fitted suit.

Marisol came up behind me and put her hands on my shoulders. "Don't feel bad, *mijo*. Men like him are the reasons our families had to leave."

That I knew. What I didn't know was whether *bad* described how I was feeling.

My phone was quiet during the night, but my rest was not. I said hello to the operator when he called with my 5 a.m. wakeup call. I had packed at 4 a.m. once I'd given up on sleeping. At 4:30, I had showered and shaved. My cell phone rang as I was removing my robe to dress for travel.

"Mike, where are you?"

"Marisol, I am in my room at the Kempinski."

There was an audible exhale on the other end of the line. "*Gracias a Dios*! Are you ready for breakfast?"

"Fifteen minutes."

"Fifteen minutes," she echoed. "*Ciao!*"

I put on a lightweight tan suit, pale blue dress shirt, and a bright yellow, orange, and green silk tie my grandfather Rivas had given me on my birthday the year before he died. I looked carefully around the room. I was leaving nothing behind. I lifted my bag and slung my carry-on over my shoulder. My hand was on the doorknob when my mobile rang again.

"*Que bola?*" It was Alejandro.

"I will be at the airport," he said in a gruff voice. He ended the call before I could respond to either his question or his announcement.

I ate breakfast with Marisol and the rest of our group, thinking of my last meeting with Alejandro and the upcoming one. Victor looked at me from another table with an alternately sad and haughty face, but did not approach me. After breakfast, our group left the hotel for the last time and waited at the curb to board our transportation back to José Marti. I went up to our handler.

"Thank you for all your help, especially with my clients' needs."

"*De nada, senor,*" he replied automatically, his eyes level with mine. But then his look became boyish and wistful. "Perhaps we could keep in touch."

Why not? I thought to myself, looking at him slowly from head to toe. His tight clothes did little to hide the trim, intriguing body beneath them. Besides, he might be useful in other ways, so my libido and ambition conspired to make me say, "Of course." I started to take out my card.

His overly self-confident smirk returned. "I have your information, Mike. May I call you Mike?"

"You can, Victor."

I think he was about to kiss me, but perhaps I have seen too many telenovelas. In any case, we were called to attention by the guide, and my colleagues began climbing onto the bus. Victor said he would text me. I had no doubt he would, maybe with photos. He had most likely witnessed my disagreement with Alejandro the night before. He might even have checked my room to see if the bed had been used and how many damp towels were draped over the bathtub. Who knows in Cuba—or anywhere, for that matter?

On the bus, Marisol patted the seat beside her, and I accepted the offer. During the next half hour, we chatted about what we had seen and done during our week in Habana. Nothing was said of Cuban friends. Once signs began to appear for José Marti International, I felt a rising apprehension. Marisol noticed.

"What's wrong, *mijo*?" Then she guessed. "No! He is not coming to the airport?" I nodded. She sat up straight, pursed her lips, and put her hand on her chest like a pledge. "I will not leave your side!" And she was true to her word, keeping her arm in mine once we exited the bus. We scanned our surroundings in unison, as if we were attending a tennis match. He was not outside the terminal, nor inside where we were given our tickets and our passports were returned. When he was also not outside security, I exhaled deeply. But as I approached our gate, I saw him. I withdrew my arm from Marisol's, squared my shoulders, and walked up to him. Marisol called to me, but I ignored her. She ran after me but, by the time she caught up, Alejandro and I were shaking hands. He handed me a set of three keys.

"*Régalos de mi parte para ti.*'

"Alejandro, I can't—"

He rolled his eyes. "Have no fear, Miguel. These are not to my apartment. They are to your family's house."

"My cousins?" I blurted.

"Your other family. It is yours. I have made the arrangements."

I thought about all that sentence might have summarized. I thought about the ghosts at the windows. "I don't want it," I said, pushing his hand away.

"Your family might," he said. He held the keys out to me again. "*Un régalo para tu familia.*"

"*Gracias,*" I mumbled as I grasped the keys. He did not release them.

"Does this mean you will return?"

"I don't know."

He let the keys go and chuckled. His face and body relaxed. "At least you didn't say you won't." He embraced me quickly and whispered, "*Mi amor*" into my ear. His warm breath and loving words excited my body and sent chills up my spine. I said nothing in return, although he waited. Disappointment and anger competed for space in his look when he pulled away. "*Adios,*" he said curtly. He put on his sunglasses and marched into the crowd departing the terminal.

"*Mijo,*" Marisol said softly behind me. She was holding two cups of café Cubano. I took one and thanked her.

"Now," she said. "Tell me everything."

I took a sip and began.

Because of Roses

I HAD NEVER EXPECTED to live in rural England, but here I was, buying a house. The New York law firm I'd been with for nearly forty years had relocated me to London. It happened something like this.

"Thanks for stopping by, Dan," Michael Tolbert said. He was the firm's senior partner.

"Of course, Mike. What did you want to see me about?" I asked, sitting in one of his deep leather guest chairs without being asked to. We had known each other that long.

"How would you like to live in England?"

"Am I retiring?" I asked, with laughter from both of us.

"No," Mike said, "But Charley Griffin will be, so we'll need someone to head up the London office. Since it's mainly international patents, I thought you'd be interested." At the time, I was the managing partner for the international patents division in New York.

"I am," I said, without any of the caution I was known for—or used to be known for. I had changed a lot since Bob died.

"Wouldn't you like to think about it?" Mike asked, not looking surprised.

"We'll work out the details later, right?"

Mike nodded. "Of course. I'll have the document to you this afternoon." I knew he would be more than fair, and he probably knew I wouldn't mind getting away from New York. Bob had been dead two years, but I hadn't really moved on.

He leaned back in his chair, watching my face like the excellent trial lawyer he still is. "But really, Dan, are you sure?" I nodded, and he sat forward again. "Is it a deal then?" he asked, knowing when a judgment had been made.

"It is," I told him. Then we rose simultaneously, shook hands, and agreed to have lunch on Thursday. That afternoon, I signed the paperwork. I did have second thoughts, but not enough to change my mind.

That was three months ago. Since then, I've reassigned my cases, promoted one of my associates, leased the brownstone fully furnished with Bob's things and mine, and bought my ticket to Heathrow. Now I was living in one of the firm's temporary assignment apartments in London while I found my own place.

I had decided against living in London before I got there. It was too big, too expensive, and too much like Manhattan, where I'd lived all of my life after Yale Law. Bob and I were both from small towns—his in Texas, mine in upstate Connecticut. We had decided a few years before, over scotch and a mutual midlife crisis, that once we retired, we'd find another small town to live in, close enough to the city for culture and friends but not too close. Since the London assignment was probably my last for BBG, I decided to start our Plan B early—and alone. I wouldn't stay in England of course but, for me, moving from New York had meant moving to a small town for the past seven years, so I rented a car and began taking weekend jaunts outside the London metropolitan area, looking for villages near a commuter line to London. I found the perfect place near the new express train to Banbury on the eastern edge of the Cotswolds, not far from Oxford.

Little Helms looked just like it sounded, a village with thatched roof cottages and gold color stone walls. My real estate agent drove me through the small downtown.

"It's looks like Meryton," I said.

"Pardon?"

"*Pride and Prejudice*?"

"Oh, yes. Quite."

It would take me a while to get used to the British after New York.

Past the few businesses, we stopped outside one of the cottages on a purely residential street. There wasn't a for sale sign. "Is this it?" I asked.

"Yes. Just offered. The owner died," the agent said confidingly. In America, an agent would never tell you that. In England, it's a feature.

I pulled my six-foot-two frame out of the Land Rover, stretched, and looked around. There was a lovely line of roses along a low fence across the street from us, in front of another thatched roof cottage with the same pale walls.

"It's quiet here," I commented.

"Extremely," the agent replied laconically, opening the low gate and leading me down the short path to the front door. There were no roses in this yard, just a few badly pruned bushes and a spotty lawn. I wondered what flowers and plants might have been there before and what state they had been in. Bad enough to be gotten rid of, I surmised.

The agent held the door for me. I had to stoop to enter but, once inside, the ceilings were high enough. "I'd have to fix that," I mentioned to her, referring to the doorway. She looked alarmed.

We went from room to room, me alternately hitting my head or remembering to stoop through each portal. I began to think of looking elsewhere, but then I saw the kitchen. I am a sucker for kitchens.

"Well, this is pretty," I said, imagining the new Viking range I'd buy and remembering our island table with a ceramic top I'd left in New York. The multi-paned windows on either side of the back door were large and bereft of curtains, which let the strong midday sun rush in, filling the room with light. I looked out the windows at a backyard as empty as the front. Oh, well. I was sure England had landscapers.

"I am interested," I said hesitantly, thinking of the doorways.

"Oh, good!" the agent said, with the first bit of enthusiasm I'd heard come out of her mouth. "Let's discuss it over lunch, shall we?" I followed her out of the house and turned immediately to look at the cottage again. It was really quite the postcard image. I could imagine my friends talking.

"Yes," I said with more assurance. "I'm very interested."

She held the gate for me. As I passed through, I heard particular sounds from across the street and looked up. A man was snipping at the roses with a pair of clippers. It seemed strange that I could hear such a small sound.

"Hello," I called, and the man turned around. His front was older than his back. I waved and, uncertainly, he waggled his clippers at me. A smile slowly spread across his face, a very nice smile. We stared across the street the usual telltale moments, recognizing our mutual sexual orientation.

He was in his seventies, probably. He had the look of someone formerly handsome, but now the jaws were sagging, and there was definitely a gullet. The hair was thinning but not receding. His cheeks were rosy and lightly tanned. Anyone not under 30 would still call him a handsome man. I crossed the street, leaving the agent audibly huffing.

"Hello," I said, extending my right hand. "I'm Dan Evans." His eyes were blue, the clearest blue.

"Martin Sinjin," he replied, accepting my hand. His grip was strong. He felt like a man who'd done more than compose opening arguments on a computer most of his life.

"Sinjin?" I asked, in spite of myself.

Martin laughed, a lovely rumble from his chest, which did not look half bad for a man his age. "Saint John," he explained.

"Oh, Saint John," I said, as if I understood. One thing I did understand however; I liked holding Martin Sinjin's hand. I looked at his face more closely, past the wrinkles and aging skin. He looked at our hands. Reluctantly, I let his go.

"I'm thinking about buying the place across from you," I said, making conversation. Martin looked at it.

"The Marley house? She died, you know."

"I know," I assured him. "The kitchen's quite lovely though."

"You like cooking then?" Martin asked, his eyes twinkling with a mesmerizing sparkle.

"Oh, yes," I answered, captivated by the twinkle, until I heard the agent clear her throat distinctly behind me. We both looked at her, and she attempted a grim smile. "Hmm," I said in her direction before turning back to Martin. "I better go."

"Is that your wife?" he asked, his smile uncertain now.

"Oh, no. It's the real estate agent. I'm not married."

His smile became certain again, and he accepted another handshake, although it became more of a clasp than a shake. "Well, then," he said while we held hands. "Very glad to meet you, Daniel. We'll hope to see you again soon."

We, I wondered? Was he married? He didn't seem like a man with a wife. Maybe it was another man. I wanted to ask but made myself not.

"Well, I better not keep the real estate broker waiting any longer," I said, not really caring whether I did or not. Her commission would be her just reward.

"Your estate agent," he corrected, using the British term. "No, I suppose not. Goodbye then."

I walked away humming, looking forward to being his neighbor.

The agent and I closed the deal over lunch, except for the final paperwork, and, when she drove the Land Rover back to Banbury, both of us were happier than on the trip out.

The buying process took much less time than in America. In just three weekends, I picked up a rental car, took the M40 to Banbury, collected my keys from the estate office, and drove the 10 miles to my new house. I parked in my new driveway, realizing I hadn't even opened the detached garage on my first visit. I looked across the street for Martin, but he wasn't anywhere in sight. I thought about him as I stuck the key in the lock and entered my new home.

"Ouch!" Damn, I really was going to have to do something about the doors. I thought of Martin again. He was tall, too. How did he handle these 18th century entrances and archways?

I went through the rooms again, feeling distracted, hitting my head almost every time. I imagined furniture in each and people visiting. The couch would be there. For some reason, I saw Martin sitting on one end of it, reading a book.

There was a knock on the front door. Martin was standing at the threshold, looking doubtful. "I saw the car," he explained, as if he thought he was being rude.

"Come in, come in!" I said, with way too much bonhomie. I ushered him inside, watching him stoop as he did, feeling first the unexpected firmness of his left bicep, and then the strength of his back. My hand rested there far too long, although I did stop myself from giving it a pat. "I bought the cottage," I informed him.

"Good for you. I'll wager the Marley cousins were glad. I'm glad," he added softly, which made me feel all sappy and suddenly warm. We stared happily at one another for who knows how long. I wondered if I looked as goofy as he did. I made myself snap out of it.

"I'm sorry. I don't have anything to sit on and nothing to offer you."

"That's not a problem, Daniel," Martin said, using my full name for the second time. I didn't correct him. I was Dan in New York; I could be Daniel here. He thought a moment. "Would you like to come across to my place for a cup of tea? Or coffee?" He thought another moment. "I think I have coffee."

"Yes, thanks. That would be great." I put my hand on his back again as we went outside. "Ouch!" I cried. Martin looked around at me. "I keep hitting my head on the door jambs. How do you avoid it?"

"You get used to it, eventually. I don't think about it anymore."

"I'm thinking about enlarging them."

"Oh," he said over his shoulder as he walked along my path. "I don't think the village council would approve of that." I enjoyed watching him walk. His baggy pants couldn't hide the fact he still had a nice ass.

My heart started thumping as we crossed the street—our street now. As we approached his roses, I could see how alike and how different his cottage was from mine. The design was the same—the shutters were even painted the same brooding green—but somehow his cottage seemed alive, while mine seemed as dead as the previous owner. Maybe it was the roses. Yellow and pink ones climbed the walls and trailed around his windows. A white variety had found its way onto the roof. Dark vertical bushes with huge red blossoms guarded the front door. And, of course, there was the yard.

There were beds of roses along the house, more beds along the side fences, and two small circles in the lawn on either side of the walk—every bush in full bloom. The symmetry was harmonious, peaceful, and calming. My heart kept thumping though as I brushed by Martin through the opened door. His body was warm through its coverings.

"Mind yourself!" he said sharply, and I ducked.

"Thanks," I said, glad not to have another bruise to explain on Monday.

My eyes adjusted to the inside light. The front room was full of furniture, crammed full. Everything was leather and dark wood, which surprised me. Given the abundance of roses outside, I was expecting Laura Ashley, not Arts and Crafts.

"Please sit," he said, indicating the furniture choices available.

"Could I see your kitchen?" I asked, realizing too late how abrupt that sounded. But I needn't have worried. Martin's eyes went back into twinkle mode, and it looked as if he were holding back a chuckle.

"I expected you might want to do that," he said, leading the way, stooping when he reached the portal into the next room. I managed to duck as well, following his example, and found myself in the dining room. I noted the heavy oak table, solid chairs, and substantial hutch with satisfaction.

"Your furniture is beautiful, very masculine," I said, wondering if that was a word too far. It was nothing like ours, but that was good. I had enough reminders of Bob without being confronted by his mid-century modern furniture in a stranger's house.

"Thank you," he said. "It took me years to find it all. Milk?" he asked, once we were through to the kitchen, both of us ducking through the door. He opened several cabinets before he found what he was looking for, a jar of instant coffee.

"Yes, please," I answered, looking around and feeling disappointed. The small table and four chairs were perfectly nice, but the cabinets, counters, stove, and tiny refrigerator all looked as if they had been there since the 1950s. I could do a lot with this room.

Martin suggested again that I sit, so I took a chair nearest the window and looked out at his backyard. It was ringed in a privacy hedge edged in roses, but the way was open across the lawn, delayed only by two lawn chairs. Two. I was dying to ask. Instead, I told him I was furniture shopping.

"I should buy a bed first, I guess," I mused. I had a list but hadn't set my priorities. I noticed Martin blushing a little under his summer tan. "Do you know of any places I should go?" I asked.

"As a matter of fact, I do," he answered, bringing our liquids to the table. He set a cup and saucer in front of me and took the chair to my left, rather than the one opposite. Our knees found each other, but his moved sharply away. He took a sip of tea. I had a swallow of coffee. It was very bad.

"Maybe you could give me a list of addresses. And draw me a map," I said, laughing. He didn't laugh or say anything for a minute. When he did, he spoke very quietly. I had to bend closer to hear him. "What was that?" I still had to ask.

"I could go with you," he repeated, his face much redder now. "But I don't want to impose myself." He buried his lips in his tea.

"You wouldn't be imposing yourself," I said, too firmly. He looked up from his cup, eyes wide. I tried to modulate my voice. Not everyone is a New Yorker. "I mean, it would be a wonderful help."

"I have a car," Martin said. "Not as sporty as your Jaguar, of course. But perhaps it would be better anyway if you drove. Get the hang of our highways and byways, that sort of thing. I can navigate." He was sparkling again, and the blush was receding.

"Okay," I agreed, taking another sip of terrible coffee and trying not to frown over it.

"Would you like another coffee, or would you rather start?" he asked, finishing his tea.

"Start," I answered quickly. Maybe there would be a Starbucks along the way. "But won't your… wife mind?"

He looked at me strangely. “I live alone,” he said, with a sad look off to the side.

“I’m sorry,” I said. I assumed I had something to apologize for.

“You needn’t be. My friend Tom died some time ago.”

He turned to washing our cups and saucers. Without thinking, I took up the dish towel and dried. Bob and I had done this so many times together. Behavior becomes automatic.

“Thank you,” Martin said, not looking at me. I suppose he and his partner had done the same. He dried his hands. “I’ll just get a jacket,” he said, leaving the room. I looked around his kitchen again. Yes, I could do a lot with this space, I repeated to myself.

We drove along narrow roads, over low hills, and down green valleys through towns larger than Little Helms and some smaller. It was such a sunny day I left the top down on the Jag. Martin gave directions, which were often emphatic. Turn here! Stop! Left, now!

Early in the day, I found a deco trundle bed I absolutely loved, although I hadn’t set out to buy one. It was aged golden oak, with curling arms and arching back. In the middle of the headboard was a large single rose carved in bas-relief into the wood. Deco had always appealed to me, but Martin discouraged me from buying it.

“You need a master bed first, didn’t you say? And a couch and chairs?”

“And a dinette,” I added, in case he’d forgotten. Martin winced at the word *dinette*.

“Well, something like that,” he muttered, leading me away from the deco piece toward regular beds with matching night tables and vanities. After he became distracted by price tags, I wandered back to the trundle bed.

"I really love it," I said when I heard him come up behind me. "Especially the rose."

"Then you should buy it," he agreed, his voice soft and encouraging, so I did, my first piece of furniture as a single man in decades.

The shop couldn't deliver weekends, so Martin volunteered to receive it. I had keys made for him, which he accepted without comment. Still, I felt there had been a change of weather.

"If you'd rather not…," I began.

He straightened his shoulders and looked me in the eye. "I'm glad to help, Daniel. I had keys for Mrs. Marley too." However, he didn't offer me a set of his.

We spent the afternoon burning more gas up and down the Cotswold Hills, to no avail—at least when it came to furniture.

"Maybe I should just hire a decorator," I suggested.

Martin looked askance at me. "That would be cheating," he said, with a smile and yet another twinkle. "You'll find what you want. It took me years."

"What did you sleep on in the meantime?" I asked, my mind imagining him in bed, which was a pretty picture indeed.

"Oh, I bought things to use until I found what I wanted."

That seemed very wasteful to the Yankee in me. I started to say so but stifled myself because Martin was staring into the distance, his gears plainly turning. "Where are you staying tonight?" he asked, looking me in the eye again.

"Banbury," I answered. "There are plenty of inns." But I admitted I didn't have a reservation.

His gears started shifting again. “Why don’t you stay with me? I have the spare room, just like yours in fact. Then, we could go out again tomorrow. There are quite a number of other places nearby.” I found that hard to believe, since we’d been to so many already.

“All right,” I agreed, without two thoughts together. “Thank you very much.” I turned the Jaguar for home, under Martin’s directions.

He had me pull into his driveway, between roses on either side. I put the top up on the Jag and looked across at my house. It was forlorn and dark. “Soon,” I promised it.

“What did you say?” Martin asked, helping me snap the top into place.

“Nothing,” I told him. I opened the trunk and removed my bag. He tried to take it from me, but I would the tussle of manners.

His guest room was as crammed with furniture as the rest of the house, excluding the oddly barren kitchen. He fished a luggage stand out from somewhere, and I hoisted my suitcase onto it.

“You can hang everything up in the armoire,” he said. “I think there are hangers.” He checked and said, “Yes, there are,” leaving the armoire door open for me. Only then did I realize a fact of his house and mine: neither had many closets. I added armoires to my list of necessary purchases.

After a meal in Little Helms’ only pub and introductions to other new neighbors, we walked back to our street, talking quietly along the way. Inside his cottage, he sat in what must be his chair. There was a second chair, but I took the couch. We talked about ourselves, admitting the obvious—that we were gay—and mentioning long-term partners, forty-one years for Martin, twenty-seven for me. His Tom had died of cancer. I told him Bob had had a massive heart attack, remembering the moment. He had been in criminal law, not a good practice area for a man with a genetically flimsy heart.

It was past one and several scotches later when we said good night. The thought passed my mind just to follow him into his bedroom, but there had been no invitation, so I walked on down the hall. Our rooms were separated by a common wall. I listened for sounds from him but fell asleep before I heard any.

In the morning, I offered to make my own coffee. After hot beverages and breakfast, Martin went to church, but I didn't have the clothes or inclination for it, so I spent the time measuring my rooms with a tape Martin had loaned me. After lunch at the pub with the rest of Little Helms, Martin insisted we drive his car on our second day of furniture foraging.

"Next week, you really don't need to bother renting," he said. "I could pick you up at the station." No one had picked me up at the station since Bob died and I'd sold the weekend house upstate.

"It's too much to ask."

"You didn't ask. I offered," he pointed out. After that, there was nothing for it but to smile and say thank you.

We spent the rest of Sunday driving over more Cotswold roads and lanes. It really was a beautiful place, the essence of quaint, although I could tell maintaining the look must be expensive. I could see why Martin and his partner had moved here once they retired, and I assumed Martin was as well off as the majority of our neighbors seemed to be. People with Bentleys aren't poor.

We finished the day back in Little Helms over dinner at the pub. Martin had a pint; I drank sparkling water. It was late but still light when we walked home. We gave each other an awkward hug in my driveway, then I got in the Jag and drove like hell back to London, thinking of Martin, furniture, and the Cotswold Hills.

He sent a text on Monday reconfirming our plans. I sent one of my own the following day, just to say hello, and we began a conversation. By the time I reached Banbury Station on Saturday, my feelings for Martin had grown geometrically. The 15-year age difference didn't matter. After all, we were both on the downhill side of life.

He was waiting for me on the platform, as promised, looking handsome and sexy in loose jeans, boots, and a light leather jacket. We shook hands. I restrained myself from kissing him. Walking to the car park, I could tell both of us were aware of that and thinking our own thoughts about it.

"I've been doing some scouting for you and found some interesting things," Martin said, to break the silence. "I put a few on hold in case you wanted to see them," he added, and opened the car door for me.

"Thanks!" I said as I settled into the passenger seat. "That's great—and very efficient. What did you say you did before you retired?"

He inserted the key and started the Bentley's engine. As he backed out of the space, he answered. "Finance. I was the chief financial officer for a munitions firm."

"In London?"

He shifted gears. "No, Lancaster." I had a vague idea where that was. Somewhere north.

"Is that where you're from?"

He merged into traffic. "No, but not far. I grew up in Manchester." I asked what that was like and his explanation told me his life's journey had been far different from mine. He'd been born poor and worked his way into the upper middle class.

We came to a town we'd been through but not stopped in. After he parked in the middle of a row of businesses, we climbed the several steps to a low shop with wide windows. Inside, he greeted the owner like an old friend, whom Martin introduced as Bruce. I was a little jealous of Bruce. He was obviously gay, in our age bracket, and much too touchy-feely with Martin.

The two of them guided me to a deco armoire with a hold sign on it. It was dark oak, like the trundle bed, and had a similar rose centered at the top. "I'll take it," I told the shopkeeper immediately.

Martin looked surprised and disapproving. "Daniel, I do admire your decisiveness, but wouldn't you like to inspect it first?" I opened both doors and smelled the mustiness of an old life. The fittings were brass, the obligatory rod and several hooks. Compartments took up a third of the vertical space and drawers filled a third of the horizontal.

"I'll take it," I said again, making Bruce happy.

By the end of the day, I had said "I'll take it" to two armoires, a master bed, vanity, and two night tables. Martin caught me humming on the way back to Little Helms. "At this rate," he commented. "You'll have your cottage fitted up by next weekend."

"I still don't have anything for the kitchen or living room," I replied. "Oh, that's not true. I'm having a stove and refrigerator delivered."

"When is that?" Martin asked. He had volunteered again to accept delivery of the items I'd bought that day.

"Next Saturday."

"Then, you won't be needing me," he said, sounding irritated. I started to object, but Martin interrupted. "Perhaps we ought to buy you some bedding," he suggested, which was disappointing. I had had dreams all week of sleeping in Martin's house again--perhaps with him--but we *were* nearing the turnoff to Banbury and I *did* have my own bed now. I sucked it up and set my mind on linens.

The Bentley's boot, as Martin reminded me to call it, was stuffed by the time we pulled into his driveway. I moved to unload my purchases, including two occasional tables in the backseat. "Come in for a drink," he said. "We'll take all that across later."

We had our drink, then Martin carried the end tables while I ferried the linen, towels and a coffee maker across the street. I had bought two, one for Martin's kitchen and one for mine. I couldn't take another morning of instant coffee. We went back for my bag and the basic non-perishable groceries I had bought at his prompting. Martin made up the trundle while I put the groceries away and set up the coffeemaker.

We ate dinner together at the pub, had more drinks at Martin's house, and then I walked across the street to spend my first night in my new home. I felt the loneliness of the place, thinking it would be better once it was fully furnished, but knowing there was another reason for my feelings.

I looked through my naked windows at Martin's cottage, its lights cheerful through the sheers. I wondered what Martin was doing. Was he taking a shower? Reading a book? Listening to music? I resisted the urge to go find out.

Monday at work, my deputy convinced me to take some time off to do the necessaries. "You'll need to have a phone connected, cable, internet, and the like," she said. I wondered if Little Helms had cable. Surprisingly, it did. I sent an email to Martin, letting him know I'd be staying the whole week following.

He emailed back, "Good. You can help me deadhead the roses." I bought some gardening gloves and a wide-brimmed straw hat, but when I arrived in another Jaguar, the roses had already been thoroughly manicured. "I was joking, Daniel," Martin said but, when he saw my disappointment, added, "Another time then. Heaven knows they need it frequently this time of year." Then he mentioned the Jaguar.

"You didn't need to rent again, Daniel," he said, staring at it unhappily. I felt guilty as I explained nine days of driving seemed like too much to expect. "It wouldn't have been," Martin replied, with a closed look that said our discussion was over.

The master bedroom furniture had all been delivered. Martin had seen to its placement, but helped me change things around without complaint. When the Viking and the Frigidaire appeared on Saturday morning with two burly young men, Martin expressed amazement at the dimensions of both while the workmen wrangled them into place and got them going. "You must be quite the cook," he said.

"I'll show you tonight," I answered, wondering if the way to a man's heart was still through his stomach. Martin reminded me I needed more than appliances, like a place to sit and plates to eat on. "Soon then," I promised him.

Over the next week, I had myself reconnected to the world, bought a couch and chairs Martin had located for me, and let him convince me to buy a 'temporary' oak table and chairs set for the kitchen. I only relented because it meant I could have him over for dinner sooner rather than later.

I also bought dishes, silverware, utensils, pots and pans, and a tablecloth, thinking of all I'd left behind in New York. By the next weekend, I was ready to cook.

"Have you always been like this?" he asked me over his tea and my coffee the following Saturday morning in his cottage.

"Not really," I answered. "Only the last two years." We both left further explanation unsaid.

"You know," he began, looking out at his yard. "We really should do something about your garden. Before Mrs. Marley became ill, she kept it quite pretty."

"Did she have roses?"

"Not many. She was more the cottage garden type, dahlias and delphiniums. You know the look." I didn't, but nodded anyway.

"I want to have roses, like you," I said firmly.

"I'll have competition then at the village garden show," he said, holding his hands up in mock fear. Then he gave me one of his looks and asked, "Would you like to start today? We'll have to prepare the soil first."

"No," I said, meditatively. "Today, I am going to cook." Martin raised an eyebrow, but not an objection.

I went shopping in Little Helms' 'downtown,' such as it was, determined to make a meal with local provisions, rather than driving into Banbury. In the end, I went with steaks and potatoes, which I was sure Martin liked, and a complicated salad and multi-berry pie baked with my own hands. I found a good red wine and a bottle of Glenfiddich.

When we sat down after drinks, Martin exclaimed, "You really are a chef, Daniel!"

"Not really," I said. "This is nothing."

"Well, it's something to me," he said, sipping his wine. "This Bordeaux isn't bad, by the way. You purchased it in Little Helms?"

"At Raleigh's," I said, taking a sip. "But I'm sure I could have found something much better at Burrell's," naming his favorite wine shop in Banbury. "It'll be easier when I have my own car. Renting is so expensive, and I hate to bother you.

"It's not a bother," he said, taking another drink of wine and a first bite of steak. "Delicious," he said, cutting another piece.

After dinner, we had more scotch and I at least got very high, high enough to ask Martin to spend the night with me.

"Daniel," he began, which did not bode well. "I do like you—very much—and, admittedly, it's been a while since I've taken the motor out for a spin, but it's still early days, don't you think?"

After that and several sputtering attempts at conversation, I watched Martin leave twenty minutes later. I made myself lock the door and take our glasses into the kitchen, where I made myself wash, dry, and put them away. And finally, I made myself go to bed, alone.

Text and email conversation, however, resumed between us and the next weekend there he was again, waiting for me on the platform in a pale blue polo and baggy khakis. "Are you ready to venture forth to the garden center?" he asked, trying to take my bag. I nodded eagerly, thinking of roses, but when I mentioned them, Martin said it was still "quite too early." At the garden center, he kept going on about soil amendments while tossing huge bags of them onto our dolly. I worried that he was overexerting himself, but he waved my concern away.

"Dr. Fetting has certified me good for at least another twenty years or so. No need to worry, Daniel," he said cheerfully. I did the math. In twenty years, I'd be seventy-eight and Martin ninety-three. Somehow, it seemed less far apart than the ages we were now.

We went home with the Bentley's boot and backseat well stuffed, changed into work clothes—or 'togs,' as Martin called them—and began digging up my front yard according to a plan we'd devised over social media during the week. I began sweating and removed my shirt. Mrs. Haines walked by soon after and gave a double take at my partial nudity. I waved a gloved hand at her and said good morning cheerfully.

Martin's t-shirt was soon as drenched as mine had been. "Why don't you just take your shirt off?" I suggested, straightening up, conscious I was probably displaying myself for him.

"Love to, but it's just not done—not in Little Helms at least." He resumed digging, and I pulled my shirt back on. When Mrs. Haines walked by again on her route back from the shops, she noted my covered torso with a nod of her head and a satisfied "humphf."

Martin and worked until noon, retired to our own bathrooms to shower, and then had lunch at the Atterbys' café. "Hear you've been gardening, Mr. McAvoy," Martha Atterby said, trying not to smile too broadly.

"Yes," I agreed.

"From what I hear, it was quite the show." She burst into laughter and walked back to the kitchen as quickly as her arthritic knees would allow.

"It was only my upper body, for chrissakes," I said to the room in general. There were negative murmurs. Apparently, people didn't like the name of the lord taken in vain. I looked at Martin and mumbled an apology.

"Nothing to be sorry for, Daniel. You've quite a nice upper body," he said *sotto voce* into his chips.

Two weeks later, I drove my new Range Rover from London, navigating the M40 without mishap. When I pulled into my driveway, I left the car out and walked across to Martin's. He opened the door before I opened his gate.

"Thanks for the text. I've been expecting you."

"Come see the car," I said, turning back across the street.

"Not a Jaguar then?" Martin said as he came up to me and the car. "I was hoping for a convertible, at least."

"I thought about it," I admitted. "But this seemed more practical."

"It is," Martin agreed, sounding like practical wasn't what he had expected from me.

I began driving myself to Banbury to catch the commuter train to London and driving myself home at night, trying to establish that a routine. The first time I missed the 6:10 from London, Martin called me at 7:30, expecting I would have driven into my garage by then. The worry in his voice warmed my heart.

"Shall I send you a text when I'm on the train or when I've missed it?" I asked hopefully.

"Oh, yes. Please do."

The texts which began to follow often, and then always, contained suggestions for a pint at the pub and dinner at my place or his. I had taken his kitchen in hand, at least to my mind. He balked at buying a new stove or larger frig but did let me duplicate additional purchases of small appliances and specialized pots, pans, and utensils. I complained about the stove from time to time while I was cooking, but Martin was good at ignoring me when it suited him.

I decided I wanted a vegetable garden in my backyard and a spot for herbs. "What about the lawn?" Martin asked in a disapproving tone. He believed strongly in lawns. He was forever commenting on the state of this or that neighbor's lawn. "They really should do something about the bare spots" or "The new rye they sowed in coming in well."

"Oh, there'll be room," I replied, looking at seeds in Banbury's Hillier Garden Centre, spelled with a final 'e', if you please. I chose root vegetables and plenty of leafy ones and decided on a small rototiller. Martin watched me work it, with a cool drink in hand, from the outdoor table and chairs set I'd found in Broughton. He refused to help me diminish my lawn.

As fall deepened and Thanksgiving approached, I thought of turkey and dressing and my friends and remaining family back in the States. I hadn't really considered going home. Well, I'd thought about it but nothing specific; my new life kept me so busy. I felt guilty when I realized this and immediately booked a flight to New York for Christmas. I let Martin know one morning over coffee and tea at my "temporary" dinette set.

"Oh," he said, and then nothing more.

"What?" I asked, watching his face. I knew his expressions so well by then.

"Nothing," he lied.

"There's something," I insisted.

He stared a moment out the window in the direction of my growing vegetables. "All right, there is something. I'm sorry to say it now, but I was assuming we'd be spending Christmas together. I thought perhaps we could take the train to London, see the light displays, and have dinner and a show in the West End." He'd never before expressed any interest in dinner and a show in the West End, even when I'd brought them up.

"Oh," was all I could find to say.

"I shouldn't have said anything," Martin said, looking morose.

"No, I'm glad you did. Very glad." I reached across the table and took his hand. It felt as warm and strong as ever, but there was something else now, a tingle crawling up my arm towards my heart. I wanted so badly to suggest the bedroom again, but it was Wednesday morning. There was a train to catch and an office to run. I began to look forward to retirement as I hadn't in years—two and a half, to be exact.

"You'll miss your train," he said quietly.

"I can't."

"I know," he answered, looking down. I lifted his chin, feeling the extra flesh there, and kissed his lips, leaving an imprint I hoped he'd remember for the rest of the day.

"Well," he said, gasping a little after I let him go.

"See you tonight," I said and rose slowly, for effect. "Shall we have dinner out or in?" We ate together nearly every night now.

"Your place, I think," he answered. "I'll buy everything," he added. I knew what that meant—more steaks, potatoes, and a grudging green salad, but a very, very good bottle of red wine.

I thought about him all day and put some of those thoughts in writing on my phone. He responded with just as much anticipation. I made sure I caught the 6:10, no matter what crisis or case needed attending to. When I reached our street, I noticed Martin's cottage was dark, but mine was ablaze with electricity through the new pale green sheers.

"Hello," he called from the open front door as I came out of the garage.

"Hello yourself," I said, striding quickly to him and through my door. He didn't remind me to duck and didn't need to. As Martin predicted, it had become second nature. He closed the door behind us, took me in his arms, and kissed me. The embrace was strong and the kiss lingering. "Wow!" I said when he finally pulled away from me.

"I missed you."

"I can tell," I replied. "What cut of steak did you buy?"

He arched a whitened eyebrow. "You're assuming I bought steaks," he said, sounding miffed. I arched a still reddish eyebrow back. "Fillets," he admitted, which in American means tenderloin.

"Well, come on then. Let's get those puppies started?"

"Puppies?" he asked, looking confused.

"It's American," I explained.

"Oh," he said, letting me take his hand and pull him after me into the kitchen. On the way, on the deco dining table I'd found under boxes in a junk shop three weeks before, was a gorgeous bouquet of roses in twelve different colors. I knew they weren't from Martin's garden, not at this time of year.

"They're beautiful! Thank you. Where did you get them? They must have been really expensive."

Martin just smiled, gave me another kiss, and pushed open the kitchen door for me.

I made the salad to be sure there was something besides bagged greens and a lonely grape tomato on top, like a cherry on a sundae. Martin baked the potatoes, which were huge, and the steaks, which were not. We tested the wine while we cooked.

"Shouldn't we save it for dinner?" I asked as he began to pour us a second glass.

"I bought two bottles," he answered, handing my glass back, full to the brim.

I spread the new gold tablecloth and set it with dishes I wish I could say had been my mother's. They had belonged to somebody's mother, I suppose, just not mine. I brought out the candlesticks and let all six candles.

"This *is* a treat," Martin said as he brought in the steaks.

"I certainly hope so," I replied.

I helped him bring in the rest of dinner. We seated ourselves and I slid my foot under the table, searching for his. When I found it, it didn't lurch away like all the times before. In fact, it pushed back, toes to toes.

After cleaning our plates and draining the bottles, we cleared up together and loaded the dishwasher I'd purchased. Including it in the kitchen had required dismantling a section of cabinetry. Martin expressed dismay at this. "Don't worry," I said. "I'm having them all taken down and replaced." He leaned against the remaining ones, arms outstretched protectively.

After dinner, we went into the living room, Martin and I ducking consecutively through the doorway. When I raised the Glenfiddich bottle, he said, "I don't think I'll be needing that." He sat on the sofa and so did I, making sure I landed as close as possible to him without actually touching. Then, I thought, *what the hell?* and scooted against him, arm to arm and thigh to thigh. That hug and those kisses had to be signals. Tonight would be the night, the first of many, I was hoping. Martin didn't move away, so in quick order my lips were on his and his arms around mine.

After several delicious minutes, Martin pulled away. "The bedroom?" he suggested. He rose and moved in that direction, without waiting for an answer.

We began to strip. It's very comforting to see another older body revealed before your eyes, even if that body is in good shape for its age. I felt simultaneously forgiving and forgiven. We held hands, just looking, until Martin slid a long finger down my chest and smiled ruefully. "I hope you'll be patient with me," he said.

I didn't know if he meant because of his age or how long it had been since the last time he'd had sex. Either way, I understood. "Likewise," I responded.

We got into bed and, as we began to make love, it amazed me how good it felt to be with a man again. We fumbled a bit at who should be where and what should be done by whom, but we found our bearings and things progressed to a very satisfactory conclusion. Afterward, we fell asleep in each other's arms. I learned that Martin snored but not too abrasively.

The next morning was Saturday. We could have had another 'go,' as the English call it, but Martin had other ideas. He gave me a quick kiss, climbed out of bed on what I knew would be his side, and announced we were going to the garden center to buy roses.

"Martin," I said, trying to pull him back down. "You don't have room for any more roses."

"No, I don't," he agreed. "But you do. Now, get up. Do you have a spare robe, by any chance?" I let him wear mine—he has such good legs—and I pulled on sweatpants and a t-shirt. After coffee, tea, and a hearty English breakfast, off we went.

Nothing else could have gotten me out of bed that morning but roses. And roses there were. Colorful bags and tall rectangular plastic pots filled the outdoor sales area at Hillier's. I dove in, making my selections based on color and fragrance. Martin amended them according to vigor, disease resistance, height, and breadth.

"We'll start with these, I think," he said when our dolly was full of potted specimens. He had shunned the bags. "It's a bit early for planting, but we'll fix plenty of mulch around the roots."

At the counter, he pulled out his credit card. "Martin!" I said, too emphatically, I suppose, since the bent head of the salesclerk twitched. "You shouldn't." He gave me a wink, his first as far as I had seen. *So sexy*, I thought.

At the Range Rover, I repeated my objection.

"Think of it as an early Christmas present," he said. "When are you leaving, exactly?"

"December 15th. I'll be back for New Year's." I grabbed his hand, with the sudden enthusiasm of a bright idea. "Martin, why don't you come with me?"

"Isn't it a still bit early for that, Daniel?"

"No," I said definitely. "At our age, six months is as good as a year."

He looked several long moments at me, making me doubt words. I really was a brash American. Maybe it was too early. Maybe it was too much to ask. Such a long flight. Then, he smiled. "All right, then. I'll book my ticket. What airlines are you on?"

"Don't worry about that," I told him, spreading plastic sheeting across the back of the car. When he objected, I looked around, gave him a wink and said, "Think of it as an early Christmas present." I put the first rose into place.

"Alright," he said, setting a rose marked "L. D. Braithwaite" into place on the plastic. His quick yes surprised me; I'm sure my mouth fell open. Martin closed it by leaning over and kissing me, in front of God, the Queen, and everyone else at the garden center. We each transferred another rose into the boot. "I am glad you like roses," he said, putting a pink one called Wisley next to the L. D. Braithwaite. "If you didn't, we wouldn't have had this chance."

The last two roses went in, and I closed the boot. "Oh, you think it's all because of roses, do you?" I asked, seeing the twinkle in his eyes.

"Yes," he answered, giving me another kiss. "I do."

I thought about that while we drove back to Little Helms and while we planted my roses. I considered an announcement carefully after booking Martin's ticket. I had almost decided by the time I sent my Christmas cards but just said, "See you soon.". It would make a better story in person when I introduced them to Martin.

And it did.

My roses are blooming now, another six months later on. Martin and I are wondering what to do with my furniture—or his. Two households, even just across the street, are redundant at this point. We're looking for a larger place, still in the Cotswolds, with a two-car garage—or the space to build one. I insisted we use the agent who'd shown me the Marley cottage. She'd brought me luck. So far, though, we haven't agreed on much. In fact, just two things. There has to be plenty of yard and plenty of sun. You see, it's still because of roses. And, of course, the lawn.

About the Author

Richard May's short fiction has been published in his story collections *Gay All Year-a Story for Every Month*, *Inhuman Beings: Monsters, Myths*, and *Science Fiction, and Ginger Snaps: Photos & Stories* (with photographer David Sweet) and in numerous literary journals and anthologies, including the Lambda Literary nominated *Outer Voices Inner Lives.* His stories are inspired by visuals. A photo, a dream, the image of a person passing in the street begin to tell him a story, which he writes down at home on his computer as fast as he can.

Rick has worked in commercial and academic publishing in New York and California in various management positions in editing, sales, subsidiary rights, and business. For ten years, he ran his own book sales representation firm in four Western states, employing eight associates. He and his team sold books to librarians from kindergarten to college.

He organizes two monthly reading series based in San Francisco. Perfectly Queer Readings features Queer authors of books with some Queer content. It is in its seventh year. Odd Mondays considers all authors and is in its twenty-second year. Rick is in his fifth year as series organizer. He is also the founder of Word Week, a neighborhood literary festival, and the online book club Reading Queer Authors Lost to AIDS, which aims to revive interest in books written and published by authors during the AIDS pandemic.

Rick is a member of the 18th Street Writers weekly writing group and the Bay Area Queer Writers Association. He earned his Bachelor's degree from Raymond College at the University of the Pacific and studied post-graduate English at the University of Southern California, with an emphasis on the Transcendentalists of the mid-Nineteenth Century. His favorite author is Jane Austen. His favorite novel is *War and Peace* by Leo Tolstoy.

He was born in California, lived in Oklahoma and New York, and now makes San Francisco his home, where he maintains a backyard garden of nearly eighty roses. His partner is the author and musician Wayne Goodman.

Acknowledgements

THANK YOU FIRST AND foremost to my life partner and love of my life, Wayne Goodman, who inspires and encourages me and my writing. He is my first reader and, because he tells me the truth, he makes my writing better.

Thank you to the 18th Street Writers—Michael Alenyikov, Andrew Chen, Anna Mantzaris, Diane Rosen, and Bela Sas--my weekly writing group, for the constructive criticism, favorable comments, and supportive friendship.

Thank you to Mrs. Sheets, my fourth-grade teacher, who first taught me to be inspired by visuals and write stories about them. Her instruction set me on a lifelong path of using visuals as writing prompts.

And thank you to everyone who has bought my books and told me you enjoyed them. I hope you enjoy *Because of Roses* too. Please let me know.

spectrum
books

www.ingramcontent.com/pod-product-compliance
Lightning Source LLC
LaVergne TN
LVHW091045080826
845145LV00002B/631

* 9 7 8 1 9 1 5 9 0 5 0 7 9 *